Escape
—from the—
Slave Traders

Trailblazer Books

TITLE	HISTORIC CHARACTERS
Abandoned on the Wild Frontier	Peter Cartwright
Attack in the Rye Grass	Marcus & Narcissa Whitman
The Bandit of Ashley Downs	George Müller
The Betrayer's Fortune	Menno Simons
The Chimney Sweep's Ransom	John Wesley
Danger on the Flying Trapeze	Dwight L. Moody
Escape from the Slave Traders	David Livingstone
Flight of the Fugitives	Gladys Aylward
The Hidden Jewel	Amy Carmichael
Imprisoned in the Golden City	Adoniram and Ann Judson
Kidnapped by River Rats	William & Catherine Booth
Listen for the Whippoorwill	Harriet Tubman
The Queen's Smuggler	William Tyndale
The Runaway's Revenge	John Newton
Shanghaied to China	Hudson Taylor
Spy for the Night Riders	Martin Luther
The Thieves of Tyburn Square	Elizabeth Fry
Trial by Poison	Mary Slessor

Escape
—from the—
Slave Traders

DAVE & NETA JACKSON

BETHANY HOUSE PUBLISHERS
MINNEAPOLIS, MINNESOTA 55438

Inside illustrations by Julian Jackson.
Cover design and illustration by Catherine Reishus McLaughlin.

All Scripture quotations are from the King James Version of the
Bible.

Published by Bethany House Publishers
A Ministry of Bethany Fellowship, Inc.
6820 Auto Club Road, Minneapo'is, Minnesota 55438

Printed in the United States of America

Library of Congress Cataloging-in-Publication Data

Jackson, Dave.
    Escape from the slave traders / Dave & Neta Jackson.
       p. cm. — (Trailblazer books)
    Summary: In the 1860s two African boys are taken captive and
mistakenly left in the care of David Livingstone, whom they accom-
pany on his quest to find a way to stop the slave trade and to open
the interior of Africa to missionaries.
    [1. Africa—History—19th century—Fiction. 2. Slave trade—
Fiction. 3. Livingstone, David, 1813–1873—Fiction.] I. Jackson,
Neta. II. Title. III. Series.
PZ7.J132418Es   1992
[Fic]—dc20   92–11170
ISBN 1–55661–263–X   CIP
                                  AC

All the named characters in this book are real. Though greatly simplified, the story draws from events in David Livingstone's second trip to Africa, the Zambezi expedition, and concludes by incorporating elements from his third expedition. Further details on how history has been condensed and simplified may be found in the "More About David Livingstone" section at the back of the book.

DAVE AND NETA JACKSON are a husband/wife writing team who have authored or coauthored many books on marriage and family, the church, and relationships, including *On Fire for Christ: Stories from Martyrs Mirror*, the Pet Parables series, and the Caring Parent series.

They have two children: Julian, an art major and illustrator for the Trailblazer series, and Rachel, a high school student. They make their home in Evanston, Illinois, where they are active members of Reba Place Church.

CONTENTS

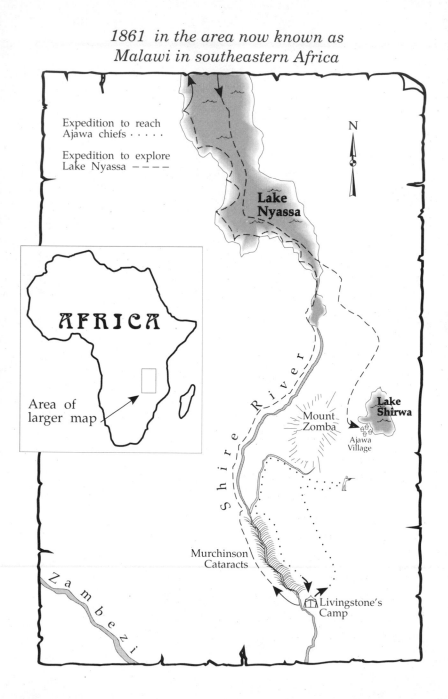

1861 in the area now known as Malawi in southeastern Africa

Expedition to reach
Ajawa chiefs · · · · ·

Expedition to explore
Lake Nyassa — — —

N

Lake Nyassa

AFRICA

Area of
larger map

Lake Shirwa

Mount Zomba

Ajawa Village

Shire River

Murchinson Cataracts

Livingstone's Camp

Zambezi

Chapter 1

Red Caps in the Mist

CHUMA! CHUMA!"
The urgent call cut through the morning mists that floated along the shore of Lake Shirwa. *Why is Wikatani yelling at me again?* wondered Chuma. He thought the older boy bossed him around too much, especially so early in the morning. What was the hurry this time? They would get the village sheep to the pasture soon enough, well before the African sun rose high enough to drink the dew drops off the tender blades of grass.

"Chuma, help. . . !" And then Wikatani's voice was choked off as though he were gagging on a ball of wool. Chuma swung his staff at the heels of the last lazy sheep. The sheep leaped ahead to catch up with the flock that stretched around the bend of the lake shore and disappeared into the mist. *Wikatani is always in a hurry,* Chuma thought. *What difference does it make whether the sheep eat along the trail or in the pasture?* Still, he couldn't remember Wikatani's voice ever sounding so urgent.

Instead of trying to push his way through the flock of sheep, Chuma ran out into the shallows of the lake to get around the woolly animals. The cool water splashed high over his body with each step until he hit a hole and suddenly sunk in water up to his neck. Chuma was a good swimmer, and there was no danger, but he grabbed quickly at the folds of his clothes to make sure the yam he had hidden there for lunch was still safe. He also checked to see that his drinking gourd still hung from the cord around his neck.

He swam strongly until his feet touched bottom again, and he waded to shore. With a brief scramble that dislodged sand and gravel, he made it to the top of the bank and plowed through the tall grass to a point where he could again meet the trail. He paused to scan the trail and listen for Wikatani. Straight ahead of him, through the fog he thought he could make out his friend, but who were the strange men, and what was wrong?

Wikatani looked as if he were fighting for his life! One man held him securely from behind while another man tried to bind the boy's feet with cords. Frightened, Chuma barely held back a scream. What should he do? Should he rush to the attackers and try to free his friend or hold back until he figured out

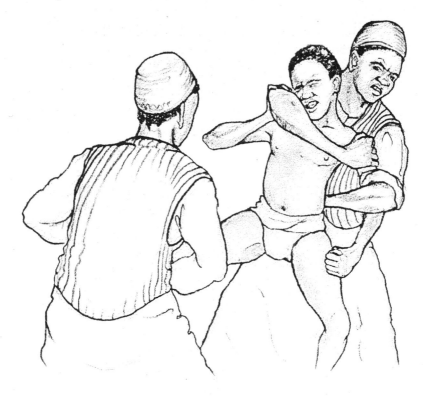

what was happening? Just then Wikatani must have
bitten the hand of the man who held him because the
man yelped, and Wikatani began yelling again:
"Chuma! Chuma! Run for help!" Quickly the man
clamped his hand back over Wikatani's mouth and
looked at Chuma.

Chuma stared in disbelief and shock as the
stranger's fierce eyes locked on him, but only for a
moment. Chuma spun around to run back down the
lake shore to their village—but he was not fast
enough. A third man who had hidden in the tall
grass jumped out and faced him with a spear pointed

right at his heart. Chuma froze in his tracks before he noticed that the man's spear had no point and looked more like a sawed-off canoe paddle with the handle pointed toward him.

Chuma thought of diving into the lake; not many people could outswim him. But before he could move, the man poked him hard in the chest with the pointless spear. It did not cut, but pain shot through his bones. Chuma decided not to make a run for it. Then the man began speaking to him in a strange language and motioning with his pointless spear. Chuma understood that he was being ordered to join Wikatani and the two strangers, so he turned and slowly walked through the deep grass to the trail.

When Wikatani saw that Chuma had been captured, the older boy's shoulders sagged. One of the men quickly tied Chuma's feet and then left both boys sitting helplessly on the ground by the trail while the men spoke to each other in their strange language.

Swallowing his fear, Chuma studied the features of the unusual looking men. He had never seen anyone who wore bright red caps or pants or vests. He knew they weren't from his tribe, the Ajawa. And they didn't look like Manganja tribesmen either. Even though the Ajawa tribe had sometimes feuded with the Manganja, they were the only two tribes in the area. The Ajawa villages were primarily situated around Lake Shirwa, while most of the Manganja villages were to the west, near Mount Zomba. So who were they?

One of the men near Wikatani stood up and raised his pointless spear to his shoulder. He pointed it toward one of the sheep that was grazing along the trail. Suddenly the pointless spear made a terrible boom, and white smoke shot out of the end. Both boys cried out with the thunder, then opened their eyes. There lay one of their sheep—dead!—while the others ran off. That was bad. The village elders would be angry at the boys for having lost a sheep, but what if the strangers stole or killed the whole herd? Fear gripped Chuma's stomach.

And what about the stranger's awesome weapon? To Chuma, it looked like the pointless spear had killed the sheep without the stranger having thrown it. "Very powerful magic," Chuma whispered to Wikatani.

"They are guns. I have heard of them," said Wikatani. "They can kill from far away."

"Of course . . . guns," said Chuma. He did not like to admit it when Wikatani knew something he did not know, even though Wikatani was thirteen and he was only twelve years old.

Then Chuma was surprised to notice the man pick up a regular spear. He could see by its tribal markings that it was a Manganja spear. The man walked over to the dead sheep and wiped some of the sheep's blood on the spear. He broke the spear over his knee and brought the pieces back and threw them on the ground near Chuma and Wikatani. Then he ordered one of the other men to pick up the dead sheep and carry it over, too.

Seeing the other man obey his order convinced Chuma that this man was the leader of the group, maybe even a chief, though they were all dressed the same.

When the other man brought the sheep back, he let some of the blood drip on the sand and grass around the area where the boys were bound. Chuma did not understand these strange actions, but it was getting scarier by the moment. Were they performing some kind of magic?

Next, the leader grabbed the drinking gourd that hung by a thong from Chuma's neck. With one jerk he broke the thong and then smashed the gourd on the ground. Chuma stuck his chin out at the man defiantly. He could make another drinking gourd. He only carried the gourd with its fresh water because it was convenient when he was watching the sheep on the hills around Lake Shirwa.

But the man also ripped the family bracelets from Wikatani's arms and threw them to the ground not far from the broken gourd. He gave more orders. One man tied Chuma's hands behind his back while the other tied Wikatani's behind his back, and then they cut the cords on their legs.

Finally, the leader of the Red Caps started up the trail while the other two men prodded Chuma and Wikatani to follow. *Now what's happening?* thought Chuma with alarm. *They are not stealing our sheep; they are taking us!*

One of the men carried the dead sheep over his shoulder. It was still dripping blood on the trail as

14

they walked. In a short distance, they turned off the main trail along the lake shore and marched west, away from the lake. The path was barely visible as it wound uphill through the thick grass toward the jungle.

Chuma looked back anxiously. The mist was lifting from the lake, and before they entered the jungle he could see its peaceful surface shining in the morning sun. Far back along the shore were wisps of smoke rising from their village. That was home, and they were being taken away. *No one will know where we are!* worried Chuma. *They won't even miss us until tonight when we don't return with the sheep. By then we'll be so far away that they will never find us!* Below, their sheep were wandering away from the trail along the lake front. Suddenly a hopeful thought came to him: *Maybe some sheep will wander home. Someone will certainly notice and know something is wrong and come looking for us. Or else,* and his spirits fell, *or else they'll just think we've been careless.*

As they entered the jungle, Chuma could no longer see the lake. The dew that had clung to the grass of the open fields now dripped like rain from the trees and vines overhead. Monkeys screeched and swung from limb to limb as the boys and their captors passed beneath. As the Red Caps hurried the boys along under the dark trees, Wikatani said in a hushed voice, "They had a Manganja spear. Do you think they are from the Manganja tribe?"

"I don't think so," answered Chuma. "Why would the Manganja take us away?"

"They're our tribe's old enemies."

"Yes," said Chuma, "but it is a disgrace to send others to fight your battles. These aren't Manganja, and we are only boys. What could be gained by capturing us?"

"Well, I am a chief's son," said Wikatani, lifting his head proudly. "Much trouble will come from attacking *me*. We are headed west into Manganja country. The Manganja must be behind this, and they will pay!"

"But the Manganja have no reason to attack us," said Chuma again.

At that point a Red Cap slapped Chuma on the back of the head so hard that he stumbled and fell. With his hands tied behind his back, he was unable to catch himself, and his face plowed into the dirt. Fortunately the ground was soft, and Chuma was not hurt. He quickly got up spitting bits of leaves and dirt from his mouth.

"No talking! Just march," shouted the Red Cap angrily, gesturing, and raising his hand as though to strike again. Chuma was as surprised that this man could speak their language as having been hit on the back of the head. *What'd I do? What's so wrong with talking?* Chuma wondered.

Wikatani said, "Don't hit him. He didn't do anything."

"I said, 'No talking,'" yelled the Red Cap again, this time at Wikatani. He spoke the boys' language well enough for them to understand him, but his accent was very thick. Then the Red Cap swung his gun at Wikatani like a club. Wikatani dodged out of the man's reach and hurried on up the trail. Chuma followed as quickly as he could.

By noon Chuma was feeling hungry and thirsty. Safely tucked in the folds of his loincloth was the small, cooked yam that his mother had set aside for him to eat while he herded sheep. He longed to take it out and eat it, but his hands were tied. Besides, he was afraid that the Red Caps would throw it away as they had his drinking gourd.

Plodding along the jungle trail, Chuma's thoughts kept returning to the house with its sturdy mud walls and thatched roof where he lived with his father and mother and three little sisters. He wanted to be brave, to face this difficulty like a man, like his father . . . but he kept thinking of his mother. *Who'll fix my food?* he wondered, even though he knew that wasn't his worst problem at the moment.

Chapter 2

War Drums

AS THE SUN DROPPED LOWER, its warm rays pierced the jungle roof only occasionally. But when they did, the golden beams sliced through the forest to turn various ferns a bright green or the trunk of a tree a rich, brick red.

Chuma no longer knew where they were. The country was turning hilly, and Chuma felt certain they were headed toward Mount Zomba, but he had never been this far west. Would they soon arrive at a Manganja village? He had no way of knowing, but he almost wished that they would. He was so tired he thought he would drop, and he was hungry.

Then suddenly, without any warning, they stepped out into a small clearing and the Red Caps stopped. It seemed to be their camp. There were two simple shelters made of palm branches under which supplies were piled high. And there were two other Red Caps already there, sitting near a smoldering fire while they smoked rolled leaves of tobacco.

The man carrying the sheep dropped it on the ground by the fire, and the leader gave more orders in the strange language. Soon the men by the fire butchered the sheep and put it on a spit over the fire to cook it.

The man who had slapped Chuma herded the boys over to the edge of the clearing and tied a rope tightly to each boy's ankle. The rope was also tied securely to a tree. He cut the cords that bound their wrists together, then left to join the others near the fire. Chuma and Wikatani tried to make themselves comfortable on the ground between the great roots of the tree and waited to see what would happen.

Nighttime in the jungle can be very dark; very little starlight makes its way through the dense roof of leaves. Even at the edge of the clearing it was dismally dark. Chuma and Wikatani sat dejectedly watching the five Red Caps around their small fire feasting on the roasted sheep and passing a jug of some sort of liquor. *Those men have no right to be eating our sheep!* Chuma thought angrily. Hunger kept him hoping that the Red Caps would bring them some of the mutton, but soon the men were so drunk they fell asleep.

With the pain mounting in his stomach, Chuma finally dug into the folds of his loincloth and pulled out the cold yam. He took a bite. It was *so* good . . . or maybe it was just that he was *so* hungry. He took another bite, then nudged Wikatani: "Want some yam?"

"What?"

"You want a bite of my yam?" whispered Chuma.

"Where'd you get that?" said Wikatani, groping in the dark until he found the yam.

"My mother. It was wrapped in my clothes."

"I never knew a yam could be so good," Wikatani sighed, handing the remainder back to Chuma. "Do you think we can get these ropes off our ankles?"

"I don't know," said Chuma, taking another bite and then putting the rest of the yam back into his clothes. He went to work trying to wiggle his foot out to the loop that held it firmly. But the harder he pulled, the tighter the rope seemed to hold him. "I can't get it off."

There was a quiet moan from Wikatani. "I made it."

"Then help me."

Wikatani pulled and tugged. He used his teeth to

try and tease the knot loose, but it was no use. The rope held Chuma fast to the tree.

"See if you can find something sharp to cut the rope," said Chuma.

Wikatani slipped off into the dark, and suddenly Chuma felt terribly alone. He waited a long time. *Wikatani ought to be back by now,* the boy thought, his heart beating fast. *Maybe he got lost. What if he never comes back?*

And then, as if he had never been away, Wikatani was at his side. "I can't find anything sharp. Only a few stones around here, and they're all smooth. I can't see a thing in this darkness."

"What about a knife from the Red Caps?" asked Chuma.

"Are you crazy? What if they woke up?"

They sat in silence for a while. Finally, Chuma said, "Maybe you should go for help."

"In the dark? I'd get lost for sure and the hyenas would find me."

It had been a bold suggestion, and Chuma shivered. The short time that Wikatani had been away had been enough to let him know how much worse it was to be a captive alone. But it seemed the only way. "How about just before it gets light? You could hide in the jungle until you can see and then find your way home."

"I guess so," admitted Wikatani. "But for now, let's get some sleep."

✧ ✧ ✧ ✧

The constant chatter of jungle birds and monkeys woke Chuma. He had been dreaming about his three sisters playing at the edge of the lake. *Home. Home is so good,* he thought, and a heavy sadness spread through his heart when he remembered where he was.

A faint light tinged the sky above the clearing. They had slept longer than they should have! He shook Wikatani, and they both sat up. But in addition to the jungle noises, they could hear something else: the thump, thump, thumpity-thump of distant drums.

"Chuma, listen—Ajawa drums."

"You're right." Chuma imagined some of the head men of his village beating the hollow logs that sent their messages for miles through the jungle. Their rhythms could announce many things, but this beat meant . . . . "War. It's war against the Manganja," concluded Chuma in a hoarse whisper.

"Because we're missing?" his friend asked.

"Maybe." Chuma thought for a moment. "That broken Manganja spear and the sheep's blood did make it *look* like the Manganja had captured us."

"And now Ajawa warriors will attack them."

"Yes. I think the Red Caps set it up that way. But why?" wondered Chuma out loud.

"Right now, who cares? I've got to get out of here."

"Take care," said Chuma, putting his hand on his friend's shoulder. "And come back soon. I don't like being a prisoner."

As Wikatani slipped away, Chuma could barely

see him moving through the dense jungle as he tried to get around the campsite and find the trail by which they had entered the small clearing. Then suddenly a terrible howling erupted. Wikatani must have come upon some baboons that were trying to raid the Red Caps' camp. The baboons screeched and yelled as they scampered up the vines to reach the safety of the trees.

Chuma held his breath and wished he could silence the baboons, but it was no use. Two of the Red Caps sat up and spotted Wikatani running down the trail. They grabbed their guns and tore down the trail after him.

"Run, Wikatani, run," urged Chuma under his breath, his fists clinched in fear. If Wikatani did not escape, they might not be rescued. And if they were not rescued, there might be a war, and many Ajawa would die.

Chuma wanted to pray to the spirits, but he knew the spirits didn't care. Their help could only be obtained by a sacrifice, and he had nothing to give. Then he remembered the small scrap of yam left from the night before. He dug it out. *It's my only food,* he thought. *If I throw it to the spirits, I might die. But if I don't, Wikatani might not escape.*

Before he could decide, a gun boomed in the distance. Chuma's heart sank. *Had the Red Caps killed Wikatani?* He waited but heard no more booms, just the sounds of the jungle coming alive in the morning—birds singing, insects buzzing, and still in the distance the talking drums.

When he felt he could wait no longer, he heard footsteps coming up the trail. The sight of Wikatani staggering back into camp was a tremendous relief. At least he was alive! One of the two Red Caps who followed him had cut a stiff vine and was using it to whip Wikatani every few steps if the boy did not move fast enough. The boy's arms were tied behind him. When they arrived at the tree where Chuma was tied up, the Red Caps gave Wikatani a shove that knocked him to the ground. The man was yelling at the boys in his strange language as he retied the rope around Wikatani's ankle, leaving some extra rope to tie around his other ankle, too. Then he gave Chuma's rope a big yank to see that it remained tight. Chuma's ankle throbbed with pain, the rope was so tight.

"What happened?" Chuma asked as the Red Cap went back to his camp. Then he realized what bad shape his friend was in. He was smeared with mud, and he had scratches and scrapes up and down both legs. There was a cut across his forehead that was oozing blood and beginning to swell. "What happened to you?" asked Chuma again anxiously.

"They caught me," pouted Wikatani, tears welling up in the corners of his eyes.

"I can see that," said Chuma. "But how?"

"I don't know," Wikatani said, looking away into the jungle. "I ran and ran. I knew they were behind me. I ran down a little hill and crossed a stream. I was climbing the other side when they shot at me with a gun. I did not want to die, so I stopped. When they caught me, they beat me."

Chuma asked no more questions.

By noon the Red Caps still hadn't given the boys anything to eat or drink. Chuma began to worry. He'd been thirsty before, but this was serious. His mouth was completely dry, and his tongue had swelled up so that he talked funny. His head felt light, as if he might fall over if he stood up. And Wikatani looked worse as the hours passed.

Finally, he decided they must do something, even if the Red Caps got angry. So he began to yell. "Give us food! We need water!" He knew that at least one of the men understood the Ajawa language. But when the Red Caps looked over at him, they just pointed and laughed. Still, Chuma kept yelling. Maybe their captors would get tired of the noise and give them what they needed.

One Red Cap grabbed a leg bone from the sheep they had feasted on the night before. Chuma eagerly saw that there were still some shreds of meat on it.

The Red Cap walked toward the boys, and Chuma sat quietly in expectation. The Red Cap stopped a short distance away and gave Chuma a wicked grin. Then he dropped the bone to the ground, kicked dirt on it, and said, "Hungry?" When he made a gesture for Chuma to come get it, Chuma lunged, but the bone was out of reach. He pulled hard on the rope that bound him to the tree, got down on the ground and stretched out on his belly reaching as far as he could, but the bone was still beyond his reach.

The Red Cap broke into a great laugh, and the others joined in. The more Chuma stretched and groaned, the more the Red Caps roared until they were bored with their game.

But Chuma refused to give up in defeat. He crawled back to the tree and began looking around until he found a small stick. Then, attracting as little attention as possible, he scooted back toward the bone and reached out with the stick.

It just reached, and he began rolling the bone toward him. He got it rolled half way over, then it rolled back. He tried again, but just when it was about to come a full turn, he slipped and bumped it back—even farther away! After that, he could not reach it at all.

"Chuma, Chuma," Wikatani whispered. "Try this." It was a longer stick with a little branch on the end.

Using it like a hook, Chuma was able to roll the bone back and finally retrieve it.

Back at the tree, the boys eagerly pulled the

remaining meat from the bone. It may have been too dirty even for the dogs back in the village, but they were so weak from hunger, they didn't even care. They ate it anyway, and it tasted good.

As Chuma was gnawing the last bit of gristle from the bone, Wikatani said, "Where did they go?"

In their excitement over having something to eat, the boys had not noticed that the Red Caps had left camp. "Ah, they're around here somewhere," Chuma said.

"I don't think so," said Wikatani. "I think they've left. Look. The supplies under that far shelter are missing. They've gone somewhere."

"Now's our chance!" said Chuma. "We've got to get free and get out of here!"

Chapter 3

In Camp With the "Enemy"

Try as they would, the boys couldn't make the knotted ropes give. And soon the boys' hunger and thirst became a nightmare that overshadowed their desire to escape. Wikatani hurt everywhere from his beating, and his cuts were already infected. Chuma hated the thought of dying tied to a tree. He and Wikatani lay on the ground, weak with hunger, dehydration, and exhaustion. What seemed like an eternal day of torment finally blended into the night and the boys drifted off into a fitful sleep.

In the middle of the night, something woke Chuma. At first he was confused. *What was happening?* Then he yelled, though the sound came out more like a squeak. "Rain! Wikatani! It's raining!"

Cupping their hands, the two boys caught the

sweet water, satisfying their thirst again and again. The shower did not last long, and soon they were both asleep again.

The next morning the clearing was still deserted. "Are the Red Caps going to leave us here to die?" asked Chuma.

"No, they will come again," Wikatani assured Chuma. "Some of their supplies are still here."

The water had renewed their strength, but the hunger grew worse. As the day wore on, Chuma had a thought. He reached over and picked at the bark of the tree they were tied to. Then he began ripping off the bark as fast as he could. Termites! And grubs! *Why hadn't they thought of it sooner?* Wikatani helped him, and the boys popped the insects and little white grubs into their mouths as fast as they could. It took a lot of termites, but the terrible pain in their stomachs finally settled into a dull ache. Both boys hoped their meal stayed down, but it was not their last meal from the tree.

Two days went by before the Red Caps returned to camp with dozens of new captives. Men, women, and children were tied together with stout ropes. Many of the children were younger than Chuma and Wikatani. The Red Caps frequently hit the men with the butts of their guns and slapped the women and children. The younger children were wailing with fear.

The Red Caps cracked real whips this time, not just vines like they'd used on Wikatani. The whips whined through the air and cracked on bare skin,

raising huge welts and sometimes cutting the skin
open as the people were pushed into the center of the
clearing.

Chuma and Wikatani stared open-mouthed.
"Look!" Chuma whispered as he noticed the tribal
markings tattooed on the bodies of the captives.

"They're all Manganja."

"You're right. And some of the men are wounded."

"Not gun wounds . . . spear."

The boys watched as two of the Red Caps set to work attaching Y-shaped poles to the necks of the men. Each pole was about six feet long and branched into a Y at the end. The Red Caps put a Y around a man's neck and fastened it by driving a long metal spike through the tips of the open ends of the Y. This left the man with a huge pole sticking out in front, or to his side or back. It made any fast movements impossible because the poles had a tendency to catch on things, giving the wearer a sharp and painful jolt in the neck.

"They're making slaves of them!" Wikatani said in shock. "Those poles keep slaves from running away. No one can run through the jungle with one of those things around his neck." Just then one of the captured men spit on his captors after they'd put the Y on his neck and began kicking wildly. A Red Cap grabbed the pole and flung the man to the ground without getting close enough to be kicked or hit.

Chuma stared in awe. He, too, had heard of this practice for controlling slaves. In fact, once he had seen a thief treated this way as a punishment.

When the Red Caps had attached Y-sticks to all the men, they set to work retying the frightened women together with strong ropes from one woman's neck to another's, creating a human chain.

Chuma counted a total of eighty-three captives. Several of the children couldn't be more than five years of age, and there were a few who were still in their mothers' arms. Some of the Manganja carried personal belongings—cooking pots, water gourds, and bags probably containing cornmeal or cassava root flour.

Many of the women were crying with grief and fear, their tears mingling with their children's who clung to them. But as evening approached some of the people began trying to make the best of their situation, arranging a family space to sit down and huddling everyone together. At first this activity created a great deal of confusion because of the women who were tied together. One wanted to go one way, and the next woman wanted to go another. Finally, things got sorted out so that they weren't continually pulling at one another's throats.

The children began gathering wood for fires while the men stumbled around in their neck yokes putting water and cornmeal in the cooking pots and setting them over the small fires to make the familiar porridge *nsima*.

With the situation under control, the Red Caps stayed back and allowed the captives to prepare their food without yelling and using their whips, except when one of the men got too near the edge of the clearing where he might try to run away into the jungle.

Wikatani and Chuma tried several times to talk to the new captives. The Ajawa language was similar enough to the Manganja language so that the boys could understand them speaking to one another. But the only response they received was angry glares; one woman close by spat on Wikatani.

"I know our tribes are enemies," Wikatani pouted, wiping off the spittle, "but *we* can't hurt them. Why are they so nasty to us?"

"I don't know," Chuma said, watching a Manganja girl in the glow of the light from the many small fires. She was about their age. "We are all captives of the Red Caps; we should help each other."

"Yes. We both have the same enemy now. The Red Caps don't belong here; they are outsiders." Wikatani was watching the same girl. She was pretty and not tied up like the older women.

When the girl looked their way, Chuma motioned to her to come over to them. She looked around to see

if any Red Caps were watching, but she did not come. A few minutes later she looked at them again. Wikatani smiled, and she smiled back. He, too, motioned, but she shook her head.

Then she casually walked away from her people and began gathering wood near the edge of the clearing. Slowly she made her way around to the tree where Chuma and Wikatani were tied. "What do you want?" she asked when she was within hearing range.

"Water," they both said. "And food," added Chuma.

She walked on, picking up sticks until she got back to her family's fire.

In a few minutes the girl returned with a small gourd of water. "Have they not fed you?" she asked.

"Just a bone," said Wikatani.

"If this tree didn't have termites in it and a few grubs, we would have starved."

The girl looked closely at the boys. "You're not Manganja," she said in surprise.

"No. We're Ajawa," said Chuma. "The Red Caps captured us three days ago when we were taking our village sheep to pasture."

"The Ajawa are hyenas," the girl snapped. "They attack when one's back is turned." And she grabbed the water gourd and started to walk away.

"Wait!" said Wikatani. "Why do you say that?"

The girl turned slightly and gave them a hate-filled stare. She spoke in a tone of deep anger: "The Manganja and the Ajawa were supposed to be at peace. We kept the peace, but your people attacked us! In the dark I did not see that you are Ajawa, or I would never have brought you water."

Chuma thought fast. Their people had attacked the Manganja? He began to understand what had happened.

"But it was a mistake!" Chuma pleaded as the girl

started to walk away again. "Our people thought *you* had captured us. That's why they went to war with you. They knew nothing about these Red Caps."

The girl hesitated.

Wikatani continued. "That's right. If our people had known that the Red Caps had captured us, they would have come here to rescue us."

The girl faced them again, still angry. "Why did the Ajawa think it was us?" she demanded.

"Who else?" said Wikatani.

"No; there's more to it than that," said Chuma. "The Red Caps broke a Manganja spear and left it on the trail where they caught us."

"And they spread blood all around to make it look as if we had been killed or badly hurt," added Wikatani.

"But why would the Red Caps do all that?" asked the girl skeptically.

"We think they *wanted* the Ajawa to attack the Manganja, so they made it look as if your tribe had captured us."

"But we don't know why," Wikatani admitted. "Why start a war between our two tribes?"

"If what you say is true," said the girl, "their reason is clear. They wanted to buy slaves. There are only five of them. So this was the only way to get many unarmed slaves."

"What do you mean?" asked Wikatani.

"We were captured by your people and taken to an Ajawa village. The Red Caps came the very next morning and bought all of us and brought us here."

"Bought you? With what?" asked Chuma.

"Rolls of bright colored cloth, pieces of copper wire, new cooking pots—white men's things," spat the girl.

Neither boy had ever seen a white man, but they had heard plenty of stories about them. Far down the Shire River, where it joined a larger river—the Zambezi—white men traveled on the water in their gigantic smoking canoes. Rumor said they had a village named *Tete* many miles up the Zambezi.

"Slave traders," breathed Wikatani. The only source of the brightly colored cloth, wire, and iron pots was white men. Often they traded those things for slaves.

A new fear shone in Wikatani's eyes. "Will we be sent away to the white man's land?"

"*We* won't," said the girl proudly. "Manganja warriors will soon rescue us."

"Yes. I'm sure they will try," said Chuma slowly, pondering the situation. "But they don't know where you are. They will attack Ajawa villages and take more captives in revenge—"

"And probably sell them to the Red Caps, too," added Wikatani.

The girl stared at the two boys in dismay. "Then . . . we might never get home!"

Chapter 4

The Trail of Tears

HOOT—HOOT—HOOT!
Chuma woke up with a start to the terrible racket. When he sat up, he saw one of the Red Caps walking among the captives blowing loud blasts on a bright tin horn.

Wiss-crack! Wiss-crack!

Another Red Cap followed the first one cracking a whip over the heads of the people. "Get up! Get up! Today we march," he yelled in the Manganja language, kicking those who weren't quick enough to rise.

The Red Caps then took the men to the shelter and loaded them with the remaining supplies stored there: more rolls of cloth, copper wire, iron cooking pots, heavy boxes, and bags of grain.

"Let's go! Let's go!" yelled the Red Cap, cracking his whip and letting it land on any captive who was not moving fast enough to suit him. The other Red Caps were going among the women making sure that the ropes that linked them together were still securely tied.

With the Manganja men loaded down by the Red Caps' supplies, the women had to shoulder all their own supplies. Several women had a huge bundle balanced on their head, a child in one arm, and a cooking pot or some other item in the other.

Hooting on his tin horn again, the leader of the Red Caps started off down the trail while the other Red Caps whipped the rest of the people into line to follow.

Chuma and Wikatani remained silent under their tree. "Maybe they will leave us," whispered Chuma. "Then we could escape."

"How?" answered Wikatani. "We haven't managed to get free yet. We'll starve tied up here if we don't have anything more to eat than these termites."

"We'll figure out something. I just hope they don't take us and sell us to the white men."

But the last Red Cap in the caravan stepped over to their tree and cut their bonds. "Hurry up. Catch up with the rest of them," he barked in his strange accent.

The boys started off down the trail at the back of the caravan. Children were crying, the Red Caps' whips were cracking—sometimes causing a captive to yell out in pain. And through it all, the women were trilling their grief: a high-pitched cry made by moving the tongue back and forth rapidly, creating a mournful wail. Chuma remembered his grandfather's funeral, and the feeling stuck in his throat.

The men were having a terrible time managing the Y-yokes. The poles seemed to catch on every bush, and when the caravan climbed a little hill, the poles constantly jabbed into the ground in front of the men almost knocking them over backwards.

The progress of the caravan that morning was very slow, and the constant whipping of the captives' backs made it all the worse. Shortly after noon, the strange company worked its way down a hill like a long centipede to a lush, green valley. There, tall sugar cane plants lined both sides of the trail, and the Red Caps were obviously worried that one of their captives would dart from the trail and disappear into the cane. They kept running back and forth along the line making sure every one remained right in the center of the path.

But one man did make a break for it. In spite of the cumbersome yoke attached to his neck, he spotted a small game trail going off into the cane and tried to run into the tunnel before the Red Caps saw him.

A Red Cap near Chuma and Wikatani saw the man. He laughed loudly and yelled, "You cannot escape us. Go ahead and try, and you will all see that no one can run from us." Just then the Y-pole on the man's neck caught in the cane and threw him back onto the path. He choked and coughed as he struggled to his feet trying to untangle the pole and swing it around behind him while he desperately pushed into the cane. Then the Red Cap lifted his pointless spear to his shoulder and—just as it happened to the sheep—there was a loud boom, a lot of smoke, and the runaway crumpled to the ground, bleeding from his back.

He gasped once and died.

Many of the captives screamed, and a woman who must have been the man's wife tried to run to his side, pulling other women with her by the rope between their necks. But the Red Caps beat her back with their whips. "Move on! Move on, or you will die with him," they shouted to the terrified string of captives.

Chuma and Wikatani stared in horror at the man who had been shot as they silently walked past his body. The Y-pole remained stuck in the cane, holding his head up off the ground in a half-way sitting position. His eyes were still open, and they stared, unseeing, into the sky.

"Get moving," snarled the closest Red Cap.

The column of stunned people marched on in silence except for quiet sobbing by some of the women. No longer were they trilling the traditional grief songs. Their spirits were broken.

In the afternoon black clouds piled high in the sky, and thunder signalled a heavy downpour. The rain made walking on the muddy trail difficult, but still the downpour was welcomed by many of the captives. They had been traveling since the Red Caps woke them so roughly at dawn, and many had not had time to get anything to eat or drink. The heavy rain at least provided a little water. The storm did not last long, however, and soon the sun broke through the clouds to warm the travelers from the chill of the rain.

As the clouds drifted away, the march continued without relief until the sun slipped behind the hills. With night falling on the strange caravan, the Red Caps chose a small meadow with a stream flowing through the middle to set up camp. The stream was a welcome place to soak sore, tired feet that had been scratched by thorns or cut by sharp stones during the day's long march.

However, the meadow had one disadvantage. It contained very little wood for fires. The few fires that were started had to be fed with bunches of twisted grass. But the recent rain had dampened the grass so much that it made a heavy smoke and gave off very little heat for cooking—when it burned at all. The Red Caps would not allow the children to venture into the forest to gather wood. This meant that most people could not cook their food and had to make do with raw cornmeal or other tidbits they had with them.

The Red Caps did not supply any of their own provisions for their captives, so the only food for the slaves was what they had managed to bring with them. Chuma and Wikatani had none, and with the Manganja blaming them for their captivity (because they were Ajawa), no one offered to share.

Chuma closed his eyes against the sharp pain in his stomach. He felt weak all over and knew he could not walk again tomorrow without food. He sat for a long time, trying not to think, then was startled when he heard someone call his name.

His eyes flew open. It was almost dark and at first he saw no one. Then he saw the girl. She had brought each of the boys a leaf with a scoop of cold cornmeal mush on it. Both Chuma and Wikatani ate eagerly. Not having been cooked, one could not say it was real *nsima*, but it did ease the gnawing pains in their stomachs.

"How did you know my name?" he asked the girl.

She nodded at Wikatani. "I heard him call you. And you call him Wikatani."

"What is your name?"

"Dauma." The girl sat on the ground near the boys. "Do you know where they are taking us?"

"We've been traveling southwest most of the day," said Wikatani. "We should be deep into Manganja country by now. I thought you would know where we are."

"My people do not know this land," the girl answered. "They fear we are being taken to the white men at Tete on the Zambezi River. We will never see our homes again!"

✧ ✧ ✧ ✧

The next day the captives made sure that they

got up before dawn so that they could prepare something to eat, gather their belongings, and be ready to move out before the Red Caps started cracking their whips.

Several of the Manganja men invented a smart way to ease the pain on their necks caused by the Y-shaped poles. With twine woven from meadow grass, pairs of men tied their poles together. The man in front arranged his pole to extend straight out behind him, and the man following swung his pole around to stick straight out to the front. Then, with the ends of each pole overlapping, a third person wrapped twine around the poles, tying them together. This bound each pair of men together as though there were just one pole between them with a Y on each end. The invention kept the ends of the poles from flopping around and getting caught on things. Apparently the Red Caps did not think it made escape any easier, because they did not object.

That day and the next several people got sick and could hardly walk, but the Red Caps had no mercy on them. The whip fell just as harshly on their backs as on the backs of those who were still healthy.

In the afternoon of the third day on the trail, one of the men stumbled and fell. His bag of corn—belonging to the Red Caps—broke open when it hit a log. Chuma saw the corn come spilling out and dove for a handful. The corn had not been ground, but he stuffed his mouth with the hard kernels anyway and grabbed for more. By then more people were reaching for the food. Some of the women pulled others to the ground with them because of the ropes connecting their necks. Pretty soon a huge pile of people were scrambling to get a bite to eat.

As Chuma tried to wiggle his way out from under the pile, he could hear a Red Cap yelling at the people. The whip whistled through the air and landed with a crack on someone's back. It whistled again, and this time the stiff rawhide cut into Chuma's leg. He yelled, spewing the corn from his mouth, and pulled himself from the pile of people. Quickly, he ran down the trail before he caught another lash from the whip.

He squeezed his eyes hard to keep the tears from coming; a few trickled out, which he wiped on the back of his arm. Then he realized that he still had

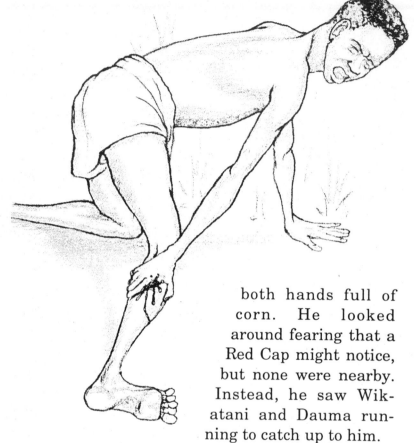

both hands full of corn. He looked around fearing that a Red Cap might notice, but none were nearby. Instead, he saw Wikatani and Dauma running to catch up to him.

"What happened?" they cried. They had been farther back in the line and had not seen what had taken place.

Chuma told them about the bag of corn ripping open. "And look what I got," he said, holding out his clenched fists. Chuma poured a little corn in the eager hands of his friends, and then put some of the kernels in his mouth.

"Aiee! Your leg is bleeding!" cried Dauma. "What happened?"

Chuma looked down. "The whip got me," he said.

Funny . . . before Dauma had mentioned it, Chuma had not noticed the torn skin on the back of his leg, but now the pain seemed to increase to the point where there was no stopping the tears. And the throbbing got worse before the caravan stopped for the night.

All night the burning ache stole Chuma's sleep. The next morning, he could not stand on that leg.

"Here," said Wikatani, "let me help you. We don't want to attract another taste of the whip."

When it was time for the caravan to get going, the two boys hobbled off down the trail near the front of the column, staying away from the Red Caps.

They had not traveled more than an hour when they came around the top of a hill and saw below them a valley with a river winding through it. A strange village lay by the river's edge. It was strange because it was not made up of the usual mud houses with grass roofs. This village had canvas tents, something the boys had never seen before, but something that filled them with dread.

The Red Caps gestured excitedly to one another, and the leader of the Red Caps got out his tin horn and began blowing on it, announcing their arrival to the camp below.

The boys saw people stop what they were doing and look up the hill to see who was coming; others came out of the tents. Suddenly, among the people coming out of the tents, Chuma and Wikatani saw their first white man.

Chapter 5

Deliverance

SEVERAL MEN FROM THE CAMP came running up the trail to meet the slave caravan. Following them came a white man.

The leader of the Red Caps was tooting his horn and waving and shouting his greetings. The Red Caps seemed very proud of all the slaves they were leading down the trail. The captives now numbered eighty-four—eighty-two Manganja (after the man who had tried to escape was shot) and the two Ajawa boys. But several slaves, like Chuma, were either injured or seriously sick and barely able to travel. If the trip continued much longer, several would die.

But to the boys' surprise, as soon as the first men from the camp met the leader of the Red Caps, they grabbed him and took away his gun. Two strong men held his arms while several other men ran on up the trail and tried to catch the other Red Caps. But seeing what had happened to their leader, the other Red Caps disappeared into the forest.

"Wha—what's happening?" asked Chuma, bewildered.

By then Dauma had caught up with the boys. She stood behind Wikatani, looking around him like a child hiding behind her mother.

"I think the white man is stealing us from the Red Caps . . . and without paying for us, either," said Wikatani. "He has double-crossed them!"

Chuma was glad to see the Red Caps run off. But if the white man was stealing the slaves, it didn't help them any; a slave was a slave whether someone paid for you or not. The white man might even be crueler. "I hope we don't have to travel anymore until my leg gets better," he grumbled. He hopped around on his good leg, keeping his balance by holding on to Wikatani's shoulder.

The black men who held the leader of the Red Caps were yelling at him, demanding to know where he had gotten the slaves, from what tribe they came, and for whom he worked.

"Quiet!" ordered Wikatani as Dauma started to say something. "This might be our chance to escape." The older boy began guiding his friends back through the crowd that was gathering around the Red Cap and the new strangers who held him.

"Wait," said Dauma, pulling away from Wikatani.

The white man had arrived at the top of the hill

and was also questioning the
Red Cap. Chuma thought Dauma was only interested in seeing a white man for the first time. He was
curious, too, but Wikatani interrupted his observa-
tion. "We can't wait," the older boy said. "This may be
our only chance to get away."

"No," insisted Dauma. "Listen! The white man is
not stealing us." The stranger was speaking
Manganja; she could understand him better than
the boys and was listening closely, trying to figure
out what the white man was doing. "He's telling the
Red Cap that taking slaves is wrong. . . . He says his
God is against slavery. . . . He is talking about letting
us go free!"

"It's a trick," said Wikatani. "We have all heard that the white men buy slaves."

"Then just look what's happening," said Dauma.

Some of the men from the tent village were tying the Red Cap's arms behind his back. Others started going among the slaves, cutting the ropes that bound the women together by their necks. As the truth of what was happening began to dawn on the weary travelers, shouts of joy spread through the column, and the people began to run forward to be released. In their eagerness, many who were still fastened by the neck rope got tangled up. Some fell to the ground, others were choking or calling for help. Dauma ran to her mother and tried to help her get untangled; then the girl guided her mother to one of the strangers with a knife.

A cloud of dust soon concealed the eager slaves.

"I don't like it," said Wikatani. "I don't trust the white man. He is evil!" He pushed Chuma away from the trail toward the forest. "Let's get out of here before he can do whatever he's up to. Look—he's got the Red Cap's gun!"

Chuma's leg hurt fiercely as the bushes at the edge of the forest tore at it. "I don't think I can keep going," he told Wikatani. "Can't we just hide here for a little until we see if the white man is lying?"

"That won't do much good if they start looking for us."

"But why would they look for us?" Chuma sat down and rubbed his leg gently. "Look. Even if the white man is planning to take us for slaves, he doesn't know how many captives there are, and since we're not Manganja, no one else will miss us, either."

Still not convinced, Wikatani sat down beside Chuma. "Well . . . most of the Manganja think this whole thing is our fault anyway, so, if we're gone, maybe that will just make them *sure* we were involved." Wikatani remained quiet for a few minutes. Then he said, "But I don't want Dauma to think that."

"What do you mean?"

"She trusts us. I don't want her to think we lied to her."

Chuma moved some branches aside with his hands so he could look out. "I don't think you need to worry about that," he said. "They really are letting the captives go. Look, they're cutting the yokes off the men."

Wikatani peered through the bushes. Several of the strangers were gathered around as the white man used a saw to cut the yoke that held one man's neck. Suddenly it gave way, and the yoke was pried off the man's neck. A great cheer went up among the men as the freed slave jumped to his feet and began dancing around. Other slaves were calling, "Me! Me next!" The white man gave the saw to one of his men who proceeded to free the rest.

As the boys watched from the shadows of the forest, several of the newly freed women and the children began gathering wood for fires and setting up the heavy metal pots to cook food . . . right there along the trail. Then the boys noticed that the white man was walking among the people giving instructions. They could hear his booming voice as he spoke in the Manganja language: "Set up another pot over here. Sure, go ahead and use the Red Caps' corn. Use any of their supplies! You need food, and they were making you carry it. So eat up. Have a feast."

A little farther up the trail the man knelt down beside a woman who was sitting in the dust with a sick child in her lap. With kind hands, the man felt the child's forehead and then pressed gently at different points on the child's stomach. He talked quietly to the women for a few minutes, then opened a large pouch that hung from his shoulder and poured a thick brown liquid from a bottle into a small cup, which he held to the child's lips.

The child coughed as he drank it and then made a sour face. The white man laughed and stood to his feet.

Chuma struggled to get to his feet. "He's not going to make slaves of us," he said. "I'm not staying here in the bushes anymore."

"Wait," protested Wikatani. "Maybe he poisoned the child. You saw how he laughed. It's better to stay hidden a little longer until we are sure."

"Maybe for you," said Chuma, "but my leg hurts, and he's a medicine man." He hobbled out onto the trail. "Doctor! Doctor!" he called out to the white man. "Would you fix my leg?"

Chuma followed the white man as he attended to other people who were sick. Finally the doctor noticed the boy behind him and turned. "What's the

matter, son? I've never seen slavers take cripples before."

"I'm not a cripple. My leg's been hurt," said Chuma, turning so the strange man could see the back of his calf. He tried to stop his leg from trembling, but it hurt too much.

"My! What happened to you?" the man exclaimed as he stooped down to get a closer look.

"It was a whip," said Chuma.

"Mmmm, yes. But it's also infected. It looks very nasty." He withdrew a small silver tube from his bag and squeezed something from it that looked to Chuma like white grease and smeared it on the wound. Then he wrapped the boy's leg with a clean strip of cloth. "There," he said as he stood up. "Now run over there and get yourself something to eat."

But Chuma didn't move. Standing next to the tall white man he took a long look. The man wore a blue suit and blue hat, like nothing Chuma had ever seen before. His face was rough, and his sharp eyes were set deep below bushy eyebrows. *Very strange*, Chuma thought. "Doctor," Chuma said, working up courage to speak, "the Red Caps tied us up and starved us, but you cut the ropes and tell us to eat. What sort of a man are you? We thought all white men took slaves. Where do you come from?"

"Sadly, you are right, young man. Many white men buy slaves, and the Red Caps have been helping them. But I was sent to Africa by God, the great God who created everyone and wants you to be free."

"Your God does not like slavery?" asked Chuma. By then Wikatani was standing beside him.

"He hates it," said the man as he stroked a large mustache that completely covered his upper lip. "If you want, I will tell you more about God later. But now I must see to the others."

As the boys gathered with some of the other freed captives around one of the pots bubbling over a hastily built fire, they were distracted by a commotion down the trail. Chuma turned just in time to see the Red Cap leader running at top speed into the jungle. Two of the men from the tent village ran after him but the white doctor called out in his loud voice, "Let him go. He'll never bother these people again."

Chapter 6

"Livingstone's Children"

WHEN ALL THE MEN WERE FREE and everyone had eaten, the people gathered up their belongings with the remains of the Red Caps' possessions and headed down to the valley. The white doctor had invited them to set up a temporary camp along the river until they were ready to return to their home villages.

When the newcomers got to the valley, they discovered that the doctor was not the only white man in the area. From snatches of conversations he overheard, Chuma figured out that the tent village was really a temporary camp, and there were several more whites traveling with the doctor, along with the black men who were working as his porters.

As the boys dropped the bundles of supplies they'd

carried down the hill, three new white men came into the little camp from the other direction. They had been up the river, bathing. The doctor went to them quickly, and the white men stood together talking seriously in low voices.

"I don't like it," said Wikatani. "They fooled us into coming to their camp, and now they will keep us as slaves. Don't forget that so far no one has tried to leave. These white men have guns and so do many of their porters. We have no chance to escape."

"You're too afraid," said Chuma. "The doctor is a *good* medicine man. My leg feels better already. I believe him."

"Well, if your leg feels better, I think we should leave tonight and go home."

"Home? That's a four-day trip! I said my leg felt better. I didn't say it was completely healed. Besides, how would we find our way?"

Just then the white men ended their discussion and the little group broke apart. They came toward the former slaves. "Gather around, please gather around," called the doctor. Then he climbed up on the stump of an old tree and started speaking.

"My name is David Livingstone, and this is Bishop Mackenzie," he said, pointing to one of the other white men. "The bishop and his assistants have come to the Shire Valley to build a mission station to tell you about the great and good God who loves all people.

"We were happy to set you free you today, and we are ready to help you return to your villages as soon as you wish. However, you are also welcome to stay here and be the first members of Bishop Mackenzie's mission station. You would be able to learn about God the Father and His Son Jesus. The bishop would teach you. You could build a village right here on the banks of the Shire River. The land is good, and we would teach you how to grow new crops, crops that you could trade for many goods. You could have a good life and help in the great work of the bishop.

"The bishop will also build a school and teach you to read and write," the doctor continued. The Manganja people nudged one another and spoke in loud undertones, shrugging their shoulders. Chuma was confused too: what did "read and write" mean? The doctor stopped, realizing that the people did not know what it meant to read. He tried to explain: "When you hear the drums, you understand the message. Right?" The people murmured their agreement. "And when you follow a trail in the jungle, you read the signs and know which animals have passed that way—a footprint here, a broken reed there, fresh droppings. In the same way, the bishop will teach you how to read little marks on paper to get the messages put there long ago by other people."

"Why would we want to learn to read such old and small signs?" someone in the crowd asked.

"They will give you much wisdom," the doctor said. "They will tell you about things and people far away; they will teach you about the one true God. God has spoken, and His words are written in a book for you to understand. Reading is very useful." He looked around the crowd. "Take time to think carefully about this offer to be part of the new mission and give us your answer in a few days."

He then got down from the tree stump, and he and the bishop strolled among the people, greeting them.

The white men and their helpers gave the former slaves machetes to cut palm branches, and the people quickly set about making temporary shelters. Chuma and Wikatani offered to help Dauma's family, but her mother said coldly, "We don't need any Ajawa help to build a hut. You have already done enough damage. Now get away from here!" And then she turned on Dauma and yelled, "I thought I told you to stay away from those Ajawa brats. If I ever see you talking to them again, I'll beat the—"

But by then Chuma and Wikatani were running down the trail away from the Manganja camp.

"She still thinks it's our fault they were captured as slaves!" Wikatani grumbled.

"It's probably hard for her to believe anything else. After all, our Ajawa warriors did attack their village and take them captive and sell them into slavery."

"But the Red Caps set it all up!" argued Wikatani.

"We know that, but how can she?" asked Chuma.

"We told Dauma, and she believes us."

"Yes, but it's not always so easy to convince adults. That tribe truly hates us."

At the edge of the clearing the boys made themselves a small lean-to. It wasn't much, but it was enough to keep off the rain.

When they finished, they went exploring. Down
by the river they both gasped when they discovered
the white man's smoking canoe. No smoke was coming out of the top of it, but it was so big that at first
the boys thought it was a strange island in the river.
There was a bridge that went from the bank to the
boat, but they did not risk going up the ramp. The
boat was so big that if it floated away with them,
they knew that they could not paddle it back. Instead, they waded into the river and touched the side
of the great boat. It was hard and cold, and when

they tapped on it with a stick it sounded like a strange drum.

"It is made of iron," said Wikatani. "But that is strange; everyone knows that iron cannot float."

"It must be filled with wood," offered Chuma. "Wood floats."

"Yes. Maybe so. Maybe so."

Just then the boys heard someone coming. They quietly slipped away from the boat and swam down-river for a short distance, then climbed out to dry on a warm rock.

✧ ✧ ✧ ✧

Three days later, when the friendly white men came to visit the camp of the former captives, they discovered that most of the Manganja men were missing. Chuma and Wikatani knew where they had gone. The men had returned to their home land to join in the fight against the Ajawa. "We could follow behind them until we got close to home, then we could slip away," Wikatani had suggested the evening the men had departed.

"Sure," Chuma had countered, "but if they noticed us, we'd be dead." Still, Chuma felt deeply homesick as the men had walked single-file out of the camp.

But now the Manganja who remained—mostly women and children—were ready to give their answer to the bishop's invitation: they would stay and become part of the mission.

The bishop could not yet speak an African language that the people could understand, but when he understood the people's decision, he began talking excitedly to Doctor Livingstone. The doctor interpreted to the people: "Bishop Mackenzie is very happy with your decision. He says that you will not be sorry you have chosen this way. You will have a fine village here, and God will bless you."

Blessings or not, Chuma and Wikatani were not happy. "How will we ever get home?" said Wikatani as the boys walked away from the gathering of people.

"I don't know," admitted Chuma. "I guess we could walk by ourselves. My leg really is a lot better now. But how would we find our way? And what if there are still slave traders about?"

"Or what if we got caught in the middle of the war?" added Wikatani. "The Manganja will not think twice about killing us."

"But I don't think we can stay here in the new village," said Chuma. "I am afraid of these Manganja. Some night they might cut our throats."

"You're right, but what can we do?"

The boys had wandered away from the gathering and without intending to, came to the white men's camp. Some of the porters were working around the camp, cooking or cleaning various things. Others lounged under trees or in their own huts, which were set up alongside the white men's tents.

"What if we moved over here?" said Chuma. "Then we'd be safe."

"They'd send us back," said Wikatani.

"But why? If we talked to the doctor, maybe we could help him. Then they wouldn't send us away."

It was an idea worth trying, and the boys stayed near the edge of camp so as not to attract any attention until the doctor came back into camp. The bishop was not with him. Wikatani hung back, but Chuma ran right up to him. "Doctor, Doctor," Chuma said, "can we help you?"

"Well, if it isn't my boy with the sore leg. How's it doing? Let me have a look." The doctor stooped down and removed the well-used bandage from Chuma's leg. At this, Wikatani came closer to watch. "That looks a lot better. Does it hurt anymore?" the doctor asked.

"I hardly notice it," said Chuma, grinning.

"Good. You don't need this bandage anymore, but try to keep the wound clean. Now you run along, and get to work on that mission station for the bishop."

"But Doctor, we want to help *you*."

"No, no, no. I don't need any more porters. Besides, you boys are a little small to carry heavy loads on the trail."

"But we could run errands for you," said Chuma eagerly.

"And we could clean things for you," offered Wikatani, "and build your fire in the morning, and—"

"And," interrupted Chuma, "we're good sheepherders."

"Sheepherders?" said Doctor Livingstone, raising one of his bushy eyebrows skeptically. "I didn't think the Manganja kept sheep."

"Oh, they don't," said Wikatani. "But we do. We're Ajawa."

"You're from the Ajawa tribe?"

"Yes. See?" Chuma said, pointing out his tribal tattoos.

"Yes, I see," said Livingstone. "Hmm. Come over here, and tell me about your village." The doctor walked over to his tent and sat on a chair. The boys had never seen a wooden chair before and inspected it carefully to see how the sticks held the man up without tipping over.

Livingstone interrupted their exploration. "Tell me where you live. How did you end up being with the Manganja?" he asked, pulling at the corners of his large mustache.

Carefully, the boys told the doctor how they were caught by the Red Caps as they were herding sheep near Lake Shirwa. They also explained how the Red Caps made it look like they had been captured by Manganja. "That started a war between our people and the Manganja," said Chuma.

"Why would that start a war?" asked the doctor.

"Because Wikatani is a chief's son," explained Chuma.

Wikatani looked distressed with the idea that the war had started because of him, and hastened to say, "But the Manganja and the Ajawa are old enemies. In almost every generation war breaks out."

"But this time it started when the slave traders made it look like the Manganja had captured you?" asked Livingstone.

"Yes," Chuma said, "and when our warriors attacked and took many captives, the Red Caps came the next day and bought them for slaves. Dauma told us so."

"Who's Dauma?"

"She's a Manganja girl," explained Wikatani.

"She's the only one who gives us any food," said Chuma. "Everyone else thinks we are the enemy."

"That's why we can't stay in the Manganja camp," explained Wikatani. "Someone will kill us—just because we are Ajawa."

The doctor didn't respond. Instead, he leaned forward with his elbows on his knees and his head in his hands. He sat that way so long the boys thought he might have gone to sleep. When he finally raised his head, there were tears in his eyes. "I'm very sorry," he said. "I'm so sorry."

"That's all right. You don't need to cry," said Chuma, unable to understand why the good doctor was so upset about their situation. "We'll be fine if you will allow us to live in your camp and help you. We won't be any trouble."

"Of course, you can stay here for now," Livingstone said, sighing heavily. "But my heart is very sad at what you have told me. I feel partially responsible for this terrible situation." The white man stood up and looked to the north, frowning. "I have come to Africa from my country to find new tribes—like the Manganja and the Ajawa—so that missionaries like Bishop Mackenzie can establish missions and schools, to tell people the good news about the great God in heaven, and His Son Jesus, who loves them. I have only recently made contact with some of your people, the Ajawa. Before my visit, the Ajawa would not allow *any* outsiders to come into their area. But as soon as I gained their trust and opened the door, other outsiders like the Red Caps have followed me and brought death and slavery with them."

Chuma and Wikatani didn't know what to say. They weren't sure that it was the doctor's fault, but they could see it was very upsetting to him.

That night in the white men's camp the boys had a good meal and slept soundly for the first time in many days.

However, the next day some of Livingstone's men intercepted another slave caravan coming through the area. This time they captured and held the Red Cap in charge and brought him to be questioned by Livingstone. It turned out that this Red Cap was the head servant for the Portuguese commander in that part of Africa.

"Does the commander know that you are buying and selling slaves?" Livingstone yelled at him.

"No, no. He does not know anything about this. He thinks I have gone to visit my relatives."

Livingstone looked at him a long time and then said, "I do not believe you. I think the Portuguese are fully aware of this terrible slave trade." Turning away, the doctor snapped, "Get him out of my sight."

"What shall we do with him?" asked one of Livingstone's men.

"I don't care."

"Shall we release him, Doctor?"

"Yes, yes. Just get him out of here."

Wikatani and Chuma followed Livingstone as he doctored and talked with the newly freed slaves, but the news they heard was very disturbing.

All the villages to the northeast were at war. Many of them—both Manganja and Ajawa—had been completely destroyed. Most of the people were either dead or had been taken captive and sold as slaves.

"The Red Caps move freely through all the area," said one old man. "They call themselves 'Livingstone's children.' But I do not know who this Livingstone is."

Livingstone winced as if he had been struck. "*I am David Livingstone*," he said as he cleaned a wound in the man's forehead. His voice hardened into a snarl. "But it is a lie. The Red Caps have no right claiming they are connected with me."

Chapter 7

A Desperate Plan

O H, GOD," MOANED THE DOCTOR as he walked back to his camp. The two boys following along behind were the only people to hear the pain in his voice. "Why, God? Why have you let my work lead to such tragedy for these people?"

The white man stumbled on a tree root, but hardly seemed to notice. Chuma and Wikatani weren't sure who this God was he was speaking to. "I came to Africa to bring the good news of your love. I have risked my life and worked hard to get these tribes to allow me to enter their territory. But wherever I go, the evil slave traders follow. And now they have the brashness to use my good name to gain access into tribes that were once safe from all outsiders!" He raised his voice until he was almost shouting. "My

God! It's not fair! What should I do?"

The boys had never heard anyone talk to a god like this, but they knew this God must be different than the gods of their tribe.

The tall man walked along in silence for a few moments, then suddenly turned to the boys as though he had been talking to them all along. "You boys live near Lake Shirwa, don't you?"

"Yes, Doctor," answered Chuma. "Our village is right on the shore of the lake."

"My father is chief of our village," added Wikatani proudly. "Often he has taken me in his canoe on Lake Shirwa."

"That's right . . . you said you were a chief's son," said Livingstone with interest. "Then I must speak to him." He turned and strode resolutely back to camp.

The boys looked at each other, startled, then hurried to catch up with the doctor. "Are you going to our village? You will take us with you?" they asked breathlessly.

The man did not answer but busied himself looking through his maps and books on the table outside his tent.

"Doctor," Chuma tried again, "can we come with you?"

Finally, the doctor stopped his rummaging and turned to the boys: "I don't see how you can. This will be a very fast trip—and dangerous, too, if all these reports of war are correct. We will be heading right into the middle of the conflict. And—"

"But this may be our only chance to return to our village!" Chuma interrupted.

The doctor gave the boys a kindly smile. "I know how you must feel—you are far away from your home and family. But I will be taking only my best porters and moving fast. However, I promise that if I see your families, I'll tell them that you are here and that you're safe. Maybe they can come get you."

The boys were deeply disappointed, and their faces showed it. Certainly their families would send for them . . . if Livingstone found them. But they did not want to wait. They wanted to go home—now! Chuma started to beg the good doctor to take them, but Wikatani put his hand out and cautioned him to be quiet while Livingstone continued to study his maps.

When the doctor looked up again, he seemed surprised to see the boys still there. "What are you standing around here for? Run along and find something useful to do." They did not move. He stared at them a few more moments, then he said, "I'd like to take you home, but . . . Say, have you boys ever seen my steamboat?" He grinned at the boys as he changed the subject. "Tell you what. I'll give you a tour of the *Pioneer*. I'll bet you've never been on board a steamboat before. I've got to go down there anyway, so come on. Maybe I can find something useful for you to do."

The boys followed the doctor reluctantly. They knew he was trying to distract them from their determination to return home with him. His smoking canoe might interest them at some other time, but if he thought they would forget their longing to return home, he was mistaken.

When they were on board, the boat seemed even bigger than before. It didn't even move when all three walked up the ramp and stepped on deck. "See how big it is," said the doctor. Chuma noted the size of the deck, but all he could think about was his home: *A whole herd of sheep could fit in back and there'd still be room for all the boys in our village to play a game up front.*

"In the rainy season, when the water is high, I can travel up the river in much less time than if I were trying to go over land through the swampy lowlands. And of course, it would take hundreds of porters to transport what the boat can carry," explained the doctor. "On the other hand," he laughed, "if the water in the river is too low, the boat gets stuck on sand bars, and it takes forever to make the trip."

A house was built in the middle of the boat while a canvas awning sheltered the front and back decks. On each side of the boat were huge wheels with paddles on them. "The engine makes these wheels go around and they push the boat along," explained Livingstone. *Just like paddling a canoe on Lake Shirwa*, thought Chuma.

"This is a very wonderful boat," said Wikatani politely, trying to sound grateful for the doctor's attention.

"The fact is," said Livingstone, "this old tub is nearly ready to sink. We've patched it up so many times, you can't tell what's the boat and what's a patch. I've ordered a completely new riverboat built in England—spent every last penny I own to do it, too. It will be taken apart, and the pieces will be loaded on a great seagoing ship and brought to Africa by the end of the year. Then we'll put it back together and have something worth traveling in. Maybe I'll take you boys on a trip in it. Would you like that?"

What we'd like is to go home, now, with you, thought Chuma, but he didn't say it. Instead he politely asked, "Where is the smoke for this smoking canoe?"

"'Smoking canoe,' is it?" laughed the doctor. "Well, there's got to be some fire before we get any smoke. Come with me." Taking the boys into the engine room, he showed them the big boilers that made the steam to drive the boat. The boys had never seen so much metal, all of it shiny like silver and gold.

"How would you boys like to polish the brass on this engine?" offered Livingstone. "It'll give you something to do."

The boys just stared at him sadly.

The doctor let out a long sigh and ran his fingers through his unruly hair. "Listen, you boys must understand one thing: my most important objective is to get this war stopped." He pointed a bony finger at Wikatani. "The fact that your father is a village chief may be of some help—if I can find him. . . ." The doctor stopped and stared at the boys for a long minute. Then he broke into a big smile and clapped his hands together as he said, "Why didn't I think of that before? Of course, of course. You boys are the key. You are the ones who can prove that the Manganja did not steal you—that there is no cause for this war. And with you along to tell your story, I can stop these rumors that the Red Caps work for me. Of course you can come!"

"Thank you, Doctor! Thank you!" both boys said gleefully.

"We leave in the morning—overland," the doctor said abruptly as he headed out the engine room door and stomped off the boat.

The boys followed him, playfully punching each other on the shoulder. "I didn't see any wood to keep this thing afloat," whispered Wikatani as they ran up the ramp.

"Well, the doctor said it is about ready to sink. That's probably why," noted Chuma.

❖ ❖ ❖ ❖

The boys were up before the sun rose the next morning. "I'm going down to the river to bathe," announced Chuma. "It seems like a good thing to bathe before such an important journey."

"You go ahead. I'm going to see Dauma," said Wikatani in a secretive whisper.

"But what about her mother?" asked Chuma.

"She won't catch me."

"You want me to come?," asked Chuma.

"No. You go on down to the river. I'll be there as soon as I tell Dauma goodbye."

"Then tell her goodbye for me, too," said Chuma, and the boys went off in different directions.

"Today we leave for home. Today we leave for home," Chuma chanted quietly to himself as he walked down to the river.

The eastern sky was a bright pink, casting an eerie glow everywhere, silhouetting the doctor's boat like a great mountain against the sky. Somehow the strange light made everything look unfamiliar, or maybe it was because today he was going home, and that made the whole world look different. But there was also an odd smell in the air, like sour smoke— not the smoke that rose in thin wisps from last night's campfires.

The boy slid down the bank to the river's edge.

The tied-up steamboat sheltered the water near the bank from the river's fast current and only small waves played along the muddy bank. Chuma jumped in the water and glided toward the side of the steamer. Two ducks scurried around the back end of the boat, trying to get away without having to take to the air.

Then Chuma noticed two strange objects bobbing in the water under the boat's huge paddle wheel. Whatever they were, they were caught there by the river's current. They were round, dark, and smooth, floating just at the surface of the water. *Probably just pieces of driftwood,* he thought. He'd seen driftwood worn smooth and shiny by bumping along the river rapids mile after mile. He swam toward the paddle wheel, thinking he would remove the logs so they wouldn't jam when the big wheel turned.

He touched one of the objects and it rolled over.

"Aieee!" he screamed at the top of his lungs and swam for the shore. He kept on screaming as he scrambled up the bank and ran for the camp.

Instantly everyone in camp was awake and coming out of their tents. Some of the men had picked up their guns.

"What's the matter, Chuma?" boomed David Livingstone when he saw the boy running toward him.

Chuma pointed back toward the river. His mouth hung open, his eyes wide. Finally he said in a hoarse whisper, "A body . . . two of them—in the river."

The men ran down to the shore. As they pulled

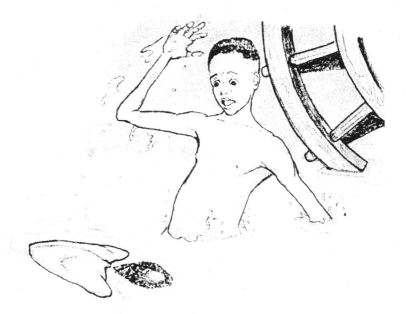

the bodies from between the paddles of the riverboat, Wikatani noticed the tribal markings and whispered, "Ajawa."

The doctor sighed. "Probably war victims. Call the bishop; we must bury them. Then we'd better get on our way. Things aren't getting any better between the Ajawa and the Manganja."

Chuma and Wikatani looked at each other in horror. For the first time, Chuma realized his own family might be in serious danger.

Chapter 8

Ambush!

THE SUN HAD ALREADY begun to slide toward the horizon when Chuma noticed the same sour, smoky smell he had whiffed that morning. The little party had been traveling at a good pace all day. The group included Doctor Livingstone, six porters—each carrying a load of supplies and trade goods—and the two Ajawa boys.

"I don't remember any of this country. Do you?" asked Wikatani.

"No. It must be a different route than the Red Caps took."

"I hope the doctor knows where he's going."

"He's got maps," assured Chuma.

They worked their way down a steep, wooded hill to a small river. On the other side, several canoes were grounded on a small beach beneath a steep cliff.

"There's a Manganja village up there that I visited when I came through here two years ago," said Livingstone as they waded across the shallows. "The canoes are still here, but where are the children? Why aren't they coming out to meet us?"

Climbing the trail to the top of the cliff, Chuma worried whether the Manganja would welcome them when they realized the boys were Ajawa. But the village was empty; every house had been burned. Chuma then realized that the strange smell came from burning huts. On the still night air, the smoke had drifted throughout that part of the Shire River Valley.

"Where are the people?" asked Wikatani.

"Dead . . . or fleeing the war," said one of the porters grimly.

In the ruins of one of the houses they found the body of an adult woman—possibly someone too sick or old to flee. They buried the body and then sat under a tree near the edge of the village while Livingstone studied his map. After a time he looked up at the boys and said in a very tired voice, "I think if we are going to find your village, we'd better turn east here and go around the bottom of Mount Zomba and approach Lake Shirwa from the south.

"We had a good march today," he announced to everyone. "My guess is that the Manganja who lived here are either captured or still on the run and too afraid to return. And since the Ajawa know this village has already been defeated, I doubt that they will return. So, let's stay here for the night."

But the porters let out a loud protest. The idea of sleeping where people had been killed and homes burned terrified them. So the party hiked east until darkness forced them to stop and make camp.

That night, however, they built no fires, not wanting to attract any attention. They also posted two guards all night. Chuma and Wikatani took their turns on guard, though not at the same time.

"What was it like? Did you fall asleep?" asked Chuma when Wikatani woke him for his turn in the middle of the night.

"Are you kidding?" said Wikatani. "I was too scared that someone would sneak up on our camp."

The next morning as they hiked east they began meeting Manganja fleeing the war. At first there were just one or two at a time, but soon they passed whole families. Some people had wounds that Doctor Livingstone tried to treat as quickly as he could. But his greatest urgency was to get to the front and make contact with the leaders of those who were fighting in the hope of achieving peace.

Around midday they came to another deserted, burned village. No dead were found, but corn was dumped out of the storehouses and spilled all over the ground. A few scraggly chickens pecked at it but flew away, squawking when anyone came near.

In the afternoon the little party saw the smoke of other burning villages. In the distance they could hear shouts of victory mixed with the cries of women mourning over their dead. They had traveled a few miles out onto an open plain with high grass, huge boulders, and occasional trees when one of the porters pointed out a line of Ajawa warriors coming down a distant trail with Manganja captives.

"This is our chance," said Livingstone. "Maybe I can reason with them and arrange a meeting with the chiefs."

But when the two groups met, one of the Manganja captives recognized Livingstone and started yelling, "Our general has come! The white man will free us! The white man will free us!" Other Manganja joined in, and for a few moments there was great confusion. The Ajawa warriors panicked and fled, yelling, "War! War!" Then the Manganja also ran off in the opposite direction, toward the distant hills, leaving Livingstone and his party standing alone in the open country, unable to talk peace with anyone.

"Why did he start yelling that I was their general and liberator?" said Livingstone, taking his blue cap off and slapping it on his leg in frustration. "Where did he get that idea?"

"Excuse me, Doctor," Wikatani offered, "but I think I recognized the man. He was one of the slaves of the Red Caps. We traveled together before you freed us."

"Of all the . . . I should have known," said the doctor in disgust as he sat down on a rock. "He was one of those men who did not stay to help build the mission. They probably told the story to every

Manganja they met. And he thought I was going to free him again. Now we'll never make contact with the Ajawa."

But he was wrong.

The white man and his companions had traveled only a short distance when a much larger number of Ajawa warriors appeared, closing in on the little group from both sides. "Down!" yelled Livingstone. Chuma and Wikatani dropped to the ground and crawled behind an enormous ant hill; Livingstone and the porters took cover in the tall grass and behind the few rocks at hand. As the Ajawa came closer, Chuma caught glimpses of movement as the warriors darted skillfully through the tall grass from rock to bush to tree. When they were within a hundred yards, they began shooting their arrows at Livingstone and his men.

Their accuracy was amazing and would have been deadly if the travelers had not taken cover so quickly. The porters had their guns ready and would have shot back, but Livingstone kept saying, "Hold your fire! We don't want bloodshed." Then he called out in a loud voice, "Ajawa warriors! We have not come to fight, but to talk peace!" But the number of arrows flying toward them seemed only to increase.

Finally, in desperation, Wikatani scrambled onto the ant hill, stood up, and yelled in the native Ajawa language, "Don't shoot! Don't shoot! I am Ajawa!" Chuma was ready to join him when Wikatani let out a yell and fell back down to the ground with an arrow through his left arm.

"We've got to get out of here," said Livingstone, moving quickly to Wikatani's side. He pulled the arrow from the boy's arm and pressed hard to stop the flow of blood. "They're not going to listen to reason."

Chuma raised his head and saw the Ajawa warriors advancing on their position more quickly, doing a wild war dance as they came to within fifty yards. One of the porters shouted, "Doctor, they are surrounding us! The trail is cut off!"

Livingstone was tying his handkerchief tightly around Wikatani's arm. "Then we'll have to fight our way out," he said grimly. It was exactly what the frightened porters had been waiting for. They opened fire with their guns and soon the Ajawa warriors pulled back.

"I hit two!" one of the men cheered. "I got one!" said another. In all, the porters claimed to have shot six Ajawa, but when the doctor climbed to the top of the ant hill and surveyed the area, no dead or wounded could be seen.

"Let's go before they return," he ordered, and the group moved warily back up the trail toward the protection of the forest.

As they reached the safety of the jungle trail, Livingstone walked between the two boys with a hand on each of their shoulders. "I'm very, very sorry," he said. "I did not want to shoot at your people."

Chuma felt uncomfortable. He had been afraid and was glad when the fighting stopped. But he had also felt angry when the porters began shooting their guns at Ajawa warriors—his own people. But seeing how discouraged the doctor looked, he finally said,

"You couldn't help it."

"Maybe not," Livingstone said. "But I have been in Africa for twenty years; I have been face-to-face with some of the fiercest chiefs in the whole land; I have been within an inch of losing my life . . . but I have never before had to shoot at an African. I have always found another way." The doctor walked in silence for a few minutes, then said, "It feels like the end of my work here. Word will spread; how will the people ever trust me?"

Chuma looked at Wikatani; pain etched the other boy's face from the wound in his arm. But both boys seemed to realize that their friend the doctor was also struggling with pain.

Toward evening the travelers came upon a group of Manganja refugees fleeing for their lives. Livingstone invited them to share their fire, hopeful that the increased numbers would be sufficient protection from attack.

"What do you know of the fighting around Lake Shirwa?" the white man asked their guests, gently cleaning Wikatani's wound in the firelight and putting medicine on it from the shiny tube.

"There is no fighting there," said the head man.

"Is it possible to get there from here?"

"No. Terrible fighting is between here and there; there is no way through."

"How do you know that there is no fighting around Lake Shirwa?" asked Wikatani, wincing as Livingstone bandaged his arm.

"Because Manganja hold all of Lake Shirwa now,"

the man said proudly. "We have taken it from those treacherous hyenas, the Ajawa." The man snarled out the last words, staring directly at the boys. Both Chuma and Wikatani shivered. Did he know they were Ajawa?

The doctor frowned. "What happened to the villages around the lake?"

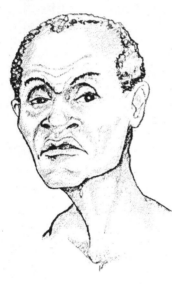

When the man answered, he did not turn to the doctor but continued staring at the boys. "All—Ajawa—villages—have—been—burned." He spat out each word distinctly. "The only Ajawa near Lake Shirwa are dead ones whose bones are being picked clean by buzzards. Soon that will be the fate of all Ajawa."

Chapter 9

The Raging River

I KNOW BOTH OF YOU want to return to your families," Livingstone spoke to the boys the next morning as they prepared to leave the camp of the Manganja refugees, "but I cannot risk repeating what happened yesterday. If what the Manganja say is true, the villages around Lake Shirwa have been destroyed, and the likelihood of finding your families there is not good. . . . And even if we did," he said, seeing the fear in their eyes, "it wouldn't be safe for you to remain in this part of the country right now."

"But . . . what will we do?" Chuma asked, disappointment sticking in his throat.

"Come back to the mission station with me. If I had been able to avoid bloodshed, we might have arranged safe passage through the war zone to reach the chiefs. They are the only real hope for bringing peace to this senseless war. But now . . ." Livingstone shook his head. ". . . we are likely to be targets for their arrows whenever we encounter Ajawa."

It was a dejected and weary band that cautiously set out down the trail. No longer did they march along with confidence. Livingstone decided that the only safe way to travel was by stealth if they did not want to have to use their guns again. So he sent out a man to scout the trail ahead, and only when it was clear would the rest of the party silently follow.

Once, when the scout discovered a party of Ajawa warriors resting beside a stream, Livingstone decided they should leave the trail and cut through the dense jungle to circle far around the warriors. It was an exhausting detour. At times they found themselves in the middle of brambles with seemingly no way out. The thorns caught and would not let go. If each one was not carefully unhooked, it would tear skin or clothes. Worse, the bramble vines were so tough that they required several hacks from a machete before they would give way.

"Quiet! Quiet!" Livingstone would whisper when someone would yelp or curse with the difficulty. "We must not announce our presence."

Finally, they came upon the trail of a herd of elephants and followed along with more ease where the beasts had beaten down the jungle in their passing.

The second night of their return trip was spent without any shelter or fire while a hard, chilling rain fell. "But Doctor," protested some of the porters, "no warriors will be moving about in weather like this."

"Good warriors will endure anything. Good peacemakers must do the same. No fires here!"

It rained most of the next day and only let up in the evening as the tired party trudged into the burned-out village on the cliff above the river.

"I still think this village is safe," said Livingstone. "If you can find dry wood that makes no smoke, I think we could have a small fire tonight. But try to shield it from view."

The porters did not want to spend the night in the burned-out village, but the prospect of sleeping in the cold, wet jungle again drove them to brave it. They found a couple huts with their roofs still in place.

Later, Livingstone spread his map by the fire and said, "I think this little river dumps into the Shire River just a few miles above the mission station. If those abandoned canoes are still down there on the beach, we could use them. It would be farther—two legs of a triangle, to the west and then south rather than cutting directly cross-country—but it would be safer than traveling through the jungle."

"Yes, but Doctor," said one of the porters, "the great rapids and waterfalls begin just above the mission station. They go on for many miles. Once we hit the Shire River, we'd be in the worst of them."

"Indeed, the Murchison cataracts are too rough to take my steamboat up, but don't you think canoes could come down quite safely?"

"Doctor, they are terrible. Many people have lost their lives in them."

"Well," said Livingstone, folding up his map, "if it gets too bad, we'll just put ashore and walk."

✧ ✧ ✧ ✧

Travel on the small river the next morning was a pleasant change from hacking through the jungle. After assuring Doctor Livingstone that they were skilled in handling a canoe, having used one often on Lake Shirwa, Chuma and Wikatani were allowed to share a small canoe of their own. Three other canoes made up the remainder of their flotilla. Livingstone and two porters were in one, while the other two canoes carried two porters each plus most of their supplies.

"We still must travel in silence," warned the doctor, and it was good advice. An hour later they were gliding through an area where the jungle hung far out over the river from each bank, almost touching the water. Suddenly there was yelling from both sides of the river just behind them, and a shower of arrows sailed after them. One arrow landed harmlessly in the bottom of the last canoe as the whole party paddled hard to get out of range.

"That was too close," murmured Wikatani as they sprinted around a bend in the river.

"If they had heard us coming and been ready, we would have been like big fish in a little pool. No one could have missed," said Chuma.

Where the small river joined the Shire River, a herd of hippopotami were swimming in the shallows. The paddlers steered well out of their way, knowing that the round, gentle-looking animals are some of the most dangerous animals in Africa. They do not like to be disturbed and can easily crush a canoe with a single bite of their powerful jaws.

But by watching the hippopotami, the travelers were taken by surprise when the four canoes suddenly swept out onto the angry Shire River. Instantly, they were shot downstream with a force that the paddlers couldn't resist. At that point there were no rapids, so the surface was deceptively smooth, but the speed with which the water moved was far beyond anything the boys had ever encountered. They could feel the powerful water drawing them this way and that with a will of its own.

Within less than a mile, they came to the rapids. They were so steep and turbulent that as their canoe came upon them, it looked like they were ready to slide down a white mountain. "Look out!" yelled Chuma, who was sitting in the back. But there was nothing Wikatani could do as a huge wave of water came over the bow of the canoe and landed in his lap with the weight of a bag of corn being dropped from a tree. The gallons of water in the bottom of the canoe made it heavy and even more difficult to handle.

"Straighten us out," screamed Wikatani over his shoulder as the current swept the canoe sideways toward a huge rock sticking out of the river. Chuma paddled hard, knowing that if the canoe hit the rock broadside, it would break in half like dried reed. But the current was too powerful; he could do nothing to straighten the canoe. And then, at the last moment, the bulge of water rising up before the rock swung their canoe around, and they shot past down into the trough beyond like an eagle swooping down on its prey. But then they faced a mountain of water. The little craft rose on the curling wave and seemed to hang in mid air for a moment and then came down, dumping both boys into the raging river.

The water around Chuma churned white with bubbles, and the strong current sucked him deeper into the darkness below. He kicked hard as he fought for the surface, but there was no resisting the cold monster that clutched him in its grasp. Down, down he went until all was blackness, and he had no idea which way was up. Suddenly something raked the length of his back like the claws of a lion, and his head crashed into stone. He tumbled helplessly over and over along the bottom of the vengeful torrent. The river was intent on knocking every bit of breath out of him.

It began to get lighter, and Chuma noticed

bubbles swirling around him. Were they his air, knocked from his lungs, or was he rising to the foaming surface? And then the river spat him out, and he flew into the air, face up with legs and arms outstretched toward the dazzling blue sky. For an instant he looked back over his shoulder and saw what must have happened. Above him was a roaring waterfall. Somehow he had plunged over it and been driven to the bottom of the pool below, then was coughed up by the river.

He landed back on the water with a stinging splat and righted himself quickly. *Where is Wikatani? Where is the canoe?* He looked around desperately. Twenty yards downstream he caught a glimpse of Wikatani, clinging to the bottom of their overturned canoe as it bobbed on down the river. Chuma took a big breath and then struck out, swimming toward his friend. *At least he is alive,* Chuma thought.

Something rose to the surface to his right. It was someone's clothes—dark blue, like the doctor's. *I should get them for him,* the boy thought. But he was too exhausted and had swallowed too much water. *I better just save myself, otherwise I might not make it.* And then Chuma realized that it was more than the doctor's blue jacket. It was the doctor himself, floating face down in the swirling water!

"Help!" Chuma yelled to anyone who might hear. He altered his course and swam for the blue patch, hoping it would not be sucked under before he got there. But the river was playing more tricks on him and kept moving the doctor away.

"Oh, God," gasped Chuma, "if you are the black man's God, too, as the doctor says, don't let him die. Help me . . . help me reach him in time." Finally, in one last sprint, Chuma reached out and grasped the back of the blue jacket. He rolled it over and pulled the doctor's face above water. There was a wound over one eye, and the older man didn't seem to be breathing. Chuma got a big handful of the white man's lank hair and tried swimming toward the western shore.

But the river bank was too far away; he would never make it. Every time he tried to take a fresh breath, a wave slapped him in the face, leaving him coughing and gasping. He seemed to take in more water than he spat out. Then, when he was about to give up, a rock island appeared right in front of him. He maneuvered to get his feet around in front of himself to catch his weight so they wouldn't crash into the rock too hard. When he hit, he got a footing on the upstream side, then reached for a handhold to pull himself up onto the slab of rock. He really needed two hands, but he was holding on to the doctor with the other. Grunting and straining, he pulled and pulled on the handhold and finally rolled to safety just as the current caught the doctor's body and swung him around downstream. Chuma almost lost his handhold. With all his might he wrestled the doctor out of the grip of the terrible current, then dragged the doctor up onto the smooth stone beside him.

The boy lay panting for a moment, but knew he couldn't wait if the doctor had any chance of living. He rolled the soaking man over onto his stomach; the doctor's legs still hung in the river, buffeted by the rushing water. Chuma sat on top of the man and pressed all his weight into the middle of the man's back. Chuma raised himself then pressed back down. Again and again he did the same. Suddenly a great stream of water gushed out of the doctor's mouth and he began coughing and choking. Chuma rolled off and collapsed on the rock beside him.

Then everything went black.

Chapter 10

The Second Journey

CHUMA AWOKE IN THE SHADE of a spreading acacia tree, its flowers giving a sweet smell to the warm air. Faces etched with concern were staring down at him. He looked from one to the other: the doctor—his clothes still dripping wet; Wikatani; and all six porters. Everyone had survived.

"How did I get here?"

"All our canoes were lost—except one, thank God," said the doctor. "With it some of the men were able to come over and take us off that island."

Chuma sat up, but quickly wished he hadn't moved. His back burned like fire.

"I want to thank you. You saved my life . . . at a great risk to yourself. But," the doctor said as he turned Chuma to look at his back, "I'm afraid I lost all my medicine and have nothing to put on those scratches on your back. Looks like you tangled with a lion," he chuckled.

"I think it was just a river—but it almost won," said Chuma.

"Well, I think you'll be all right until we get something for it. But we'd better get going, if you feel well enough to walk. It's going to take another full day or maybe even longer to get back to the mission station."

✧ ✧ ✧ ✧

In the days and weeks that followed at the mission station, Chuma and Wikatani often worried about what the Manganja warriors had said about their village. "What if our families are all dead as that Manganja said?" said Wikatani one day. Both boys had been afraid to put their worst fears into words.

Chuma thought for a long time. When he broke the silence, there were tears in his eyes. "If they are, I will stay with the doctor and be a Christian. But we do not know that. We cannot give up hope."

"Besides," said Wikatani. "The Manganja like to boast. He was just trying to scare us. But . . . we must go back and let our families know we are alive."

It was only a couple of days later that Livingstone called the boys to him while he was sitting outside his tent studying his maps.

"I have heard reports of another lake to the north

of your homeland. It is said to be a very great body of water. Do you know of it?" he said, looking up at the boys standing beside his table.

Chuma shrugged, but Wikatani said, "I have heard of it. It is called *Nyassa*."

"Yes, Lake Nyassa," mused the doctor, pulling at the corners of his mustache. "Have you ever seen it?"

"No, Doctor, but my father has."

"He has? Did he tell you anything about it?"

"Only that it is very, very long. One old man told him that if you started as a boy, you'd be an old man before you finished walking around it."

"Really?"

"He said it, but everyone else laughed and said it would take two months to walk around it—but it can't be done."

"Why not?"

"I don't know."

"That's still pretty big. I must explore this Lake Nyassa. It may be the key to stopping the slave traders."

The boys did not understand.

"You see," the doctor continued, punching a point on the map with his finger, "if we could get a steamboat onto Lake Nyassa, we could bring in the supplies and people to set up a mission station there. I could claim that part of the country for England, and it would be out from under the control of the Portuguese slavers. *Then* we could be much more effective in stopping this terrible slave trade."

"But Doctor," said Chuma, "how would you get

your steamboat beyond the rapids?"

David Livingstone shrugged. "That's why I must explore the lake. If it is as big as you say, then it has to have another outlet besides the Shire River." Livingstone got up and started pacing around his camp, slamming his right fist into the palm of his left hand with each step. He whirled and pointed at Wikatani. "Did your father say anything about a river running out of the lake to the east all the way to the sea?"

"No."

"Well, there must be one, and I will find it. The whole geography of the region demands one."

As the boys left the doctor's camp, Wikatani turned to Chuma and said excitedly, "Did you look at the doctor's map?"

"Yes. What about it?"

"We could not get home from the south because of the terrible fighting between us and Lake Shirwa. But what if we approached Lake Shirwa from the north?"

"There might not be so much fighting up there."

"Right," said Wikatani eagerly. "If we could go on this expedition with Doctor Livingstone, we could travel up the Shire River, around all the fighting to Lake Nyassa to the north—"

"From there," interrupted Chuma eagerly as he saw the plan, "we could come down to our homeland."

❖ ❖ ❖ ❖

The boys had to do some fast talking, but three days later they were again part of the doctor's expedition. They did not, however, tell him their real hopes for wanting to go along.

The Murchison cataracts that began just above the mission station on the Shire River did not allow for any boat travel. So four porters carried a four-oared rowboat as they headed north along the west bank of the river. Two more men went ahead and cleared the way with machetes. Livingstone preceded them, trying to scout out the easiest path—which was never very easy as they were always going steeply uphill. Chuma and Wikatani followed, loaded down with the heavy oars, the sail, and an awning. "When we get on that lake, we'll be glad for this sail," the doctor had said. "And the awning will protect us from the sun day after day."

When the men were exhausted, they put the boat down and everyone got a rest—if you could call it that—while all but two (left as guards) hiked back to pick up their supplies. Then everyone hoisted boxes and bundles onto their backs and carried them up to the point where they had left the boat. Then they did it all again.

On a good day, this routine was repeated three or four times.

Along the way, the boys marveled that they had ever tried to come down the river in canoes. Often they would hike for miles along the top edge of a deep gorge with the raging river at the bottom and no shore at the water's edge where they could have

sought safety or taken a rest.

Once Livingstone showed the boys the map. "The Murchison cataracts on the Shire River are forty miles long. I think the Lord God was protecting us by getting us out of that river as quickly as He did," the doctor admitted.

Soon they passed the point where their canoes

had come out of the small river onto the Shire. But it took a total of three weeks of torturous work portaging the rowboat overland before the party arrived at a point where they could safely put it in the river.

Having finally arrived at calm water, they took a day to rest, hunt for fresh meat, and prepare for the next leg of their journey.

Travel on the river the next day was a pleasant relief from the constant toil of carrying their heavy loads uphill. The water was relatively smooth, and their rowing—while hard work—made good progress.

Along the rapids they had not seen any signs of the tribal war. But that day, in the rolling hills to the east, a great pillar of black smoke rose high into the silvery sky. Since the area was mostly green jungle, it did not seem likely that the fire was accidental but probably a village that had been put to the torch.

That night they camped at the base of a cliff in a damp, marshy area. "No fires tonight," said Livingstone. "We don't want to attract any attention."

Later, as everyone slapped at the mosquitoes that would not let them eat in peace, Chuma decided it was time to bring up their plan.

"Doctor Livingstone, when we get to Lake Nyassa, won't we be almost straight north of Lake Shirwa?"

"Almost, Chuma. Why do you ask?"

"Wikatani and I were thinking that it might be safe to travel to Lake Shirwa if we came down from the north since the battles we ran into were south of the lake."

The doctor sat silently for a few moments, a deep frown creasing his forehead as he pulled at his mustache. "It might be possible," he finally agreed. "But here we are almost straight west of Lake Shirwa and we saw that burning village today. So the fighting is not only in the south. But why do you ask?"

"We were wondering," jumped in Wikatani, "whether, when you got that far north, you might decide to go south to meet the Ajawa chiefs."

"And you could take us with you to find our families," added Chuma.

Livingstone got up and walked down to the water's edge. The boys did not know whether he was angry or not. Finally, he strode back to the rest of them. "I *had* hoped to bring a quick end to this fighting by trying to reach the Ajawa chiefs," he explained. "But we failed. Since then, I've come to feel that God has a larger purpose for me: I believe we *must* establish a mission base in the interior. It's the only way to break the back of this wicked slave trade—"

"But you wanted to stop the war. Remember?" said Chuma.

"Yes, and I would still give my life to accomplish that. But I must not be shortsighted. I do not know how much longer the Portuguese will allow me to remain in this part of Africa. We must establish a permanent base farther north—around Lake Nyassa—and the only hope is to find a waterway from it to the sea. Then I can get a steamboat with supplies into the interior."

All the porters were quiet and listening intently.

"You see, as terrible as this tribal war is," Livingstone went on, "there is a more serious mission. The bishop and others like him want to bring the Gospel—the story about God's Son, Jesus—to all these tribes. Jesus showed people a new way to live with one another. He forgave His enemies; He showed that everyone—old and young, men, women, and children, black and white—is important to God. Most important, Jesus died to take the punishment for our sins, so that all of us can live with God in heaven forever."

No one spoke. This was something to think about.

"You see, the only real way to stop the slavers and the fighting is to change people's hearts. If the people hear the Gospel, maybe they will obey God's commandments and stop warring with one another and selling people into slavery."

Livingstone looked kindly at Chuma and Wikatani. "I'm sorry, my young friends. I must try for the greater purpose first. We must go on to Lake

Nyassa and find the river to the sea. Then maybe we can make another attempt to reach the Ajawa chiefs."

Chapter 11

Lake Nyassa

IN THE AFTERNOON of the next day a breeze arose along the river; Livingstone put up the sail, and they moved along even faster than the men could row. What a welcomed rest! Chuma and Wikatani had never seen a sailing vessel, let alone ridden in one. "We are like kings with invisible slaves rowing us along," Chuma grinned.

Three days more they traveled with much the same routine, rowing in the morning and sailing in the afternoon, until—four weeks after leaving the mission station—the river mouth widened and they came out onto Lake Nyassa. It was so big, the water seemed to run right into the sky. Doctor Livingstone was even more excited than the boys; he wrote the date in a little book and read it to the boys: "We found Lake Nyassa on September second, 1861."

Beaching the boat on a gentle bank, the travelers were met by hundreds of Africans who had never seen a white man before. Even the men were very curious, wanting to touch Livingstone's skin and feel his strange, limp hair.

The people were friendly and eagerly provided plenty of food for the newcomers, including fish from the lake. However, they did not speak a language that any of the travelers could understand, so communication was very difficult. But Chuma and Wikatani were impressed with the doctor's skill in learning a new language. Before the evening was over he had mastered dozens of words and could put together a few simple sentences to the great amusement of the local people.

Each day the little boat of explorers traveled farther north on the great lake and spent the evening in a new village on the shore. As soon as Livingstone was able to communicate with the people, he began telling them about Jesus, how He was the Son of the only true God, and that He had come to earth to tell everyone of God's love and forgiveness of sin. The people listened attentively, but few responded. "That's all right," said the doctor. "I planted a seed."

At every stop Livingstone also asked if there was a river that flowed east out of the lake. But every person he questioned gave a different answer. One man declared positively that they could sail right out of the lake on such a river; but the next man said, no, they would need to hike overland fifty or even a hundred miles before reaching a river of any size.

"We're going to have to see for ourselves," Livingstone said stubbornly.

But as they made their way along the shore of the great lake, trouble began to develop. One night robbers crept into their camp while they slept and stole nearly all their supplies. The most serious loss was their food and trade goods. The trade goods were important in making friends with new tribes and in paying tolls to the chiefs for permission to pass through their territory.

The next night no one met them when they beached their boat. Pushing into the surrounding jungle, the travelers found a village burned to the ground and strewn with rotting bodies. "More tribal warfare," Livingston muttered, poking through the ruins. "I'll bet the slavers are behind this, too."

Once again the porters insisted that they leave the place of death; they rowed by moonlight until they saw a deserted beach and pulled toward shore.

But no sooner had they landed than a large group of warriors ran out of the jungle, painted for war and waving their spears fiercely. "Mazitu!" one of the porters cried fearfully. As the warriors advanced, the porters immediately raised their guns. With nothing to trade, Chuma was sure they would have to resort to their guns again to avoid being killed.

"Wait!" Livingstone ordered. At the last minute he rolled up his sleeves and opened his shirt, exposing the whiteness of skin that had not been tanned by the sun. In the moonlight his skin shone pale and

ghostly. The warriors stopped in their tracks. Cautiously, one moved forward, his spear extended. He brought the tip to Livingstone's chest and drew it down slowly across the skin. The tiny trickle of blood that followed the sharp point looked black, rather than red, in the strange, pale light.

Suddenly the warriors let out a frightened cry, turned, and fled back into the jungle.

Startled, the little group stood staring at the dark edge of the jungle that had swallowed up the fierce warriors.

One of the porters finally broke the silence. "We must not continue!" he declared. "We have no food and nothing to trade for more. The next war party may not be so scared by your trick. It is time to go back."

"Yes. Yes. We must go back," the others insisted.

But Livingstone protested and there was a big argument. Finally he convinced the men to go on one more day in hopes of moving out of the war-torn area.

They posted guards that night as had become their custom wherever trouble threatened, and it was Chuma's lot to draw guard duty with Doctor Livingstone. Because they had set up camp on the open beach, no one could approach the camp without being seen. The guards did not have to patrol so much as watch over the camp in the moonlight. Chuma and the doctor chose the top of a small dune near their sleeping companions and sat down.

When all was quiet, Chuma said, "Doctor, I would like to become a Christian like you, and follow your God."

"That's good, Chuma. But tell me, why do you want to do this?"

"Well, you could have ordered those warriors shot tonight, but God gave you great courage to do a good thing."

"Yes, He did, Chuma. But what if I had not had that courage?"

Chuma thought for a while. "I still think you would have *wanted* the good thing. I think you really love the African people."

"But *why* do you think I love Africans?"

"Because you love God, and God loves all people.

That's why God sent His Son, Jesus, to die for us."
Chuma grinned, remembering what he had heard
the bishop and the doctor say.

"That's right, Chuma. And you must remember
that. Even if I completely fail to do what's right,
Jesus did not fail. Put your trust in Him, not in how
well other people behave."

They listened in quietness to the waves gently
lapping at the beach, then Chuma asked, "But, how
do I become a Christian?"

"Well, you know that we're all sinners. And that's
more than occasionally doing an evil thing like lying
or stealing—those, of course, are sins. Even when we
try hard to do good—like I'm trying to find a way to
stop the slave trade—it doesn't always work out.
And sometimes we make things worse, and people
get hurt. Then we realize how badly we need someone to save us."

"I know that, and that's what I want. I want
Jesus to save me. But how?"

"The Bible says, 'As many as received him, to
them gave he power to become the sons of God, even
to them that believe on his name.' Do you believe
that, Chuma? Do you want to give your life to Jesus?"

"Yes."

They talked some more, and then Chuma prayed.
The next morning before setting out, Doctor
Livingstone baptized Chuma in the lake as a new
Christian while the others watched.

✧ ✧ ✧ ✧

That night, when the explorers stopped, they were met by local people who laughed at them and thought they were fleeing from the Mazitu. For some reason—Chuma never found out why—a shoving match started between the porters and the villagers that soon broke into a fight with sticks. Livingstone did his best to stop it, and the local people finally withdrew sullenly. The travelers made camp, but decided not to sleep by the fire. Instead, they made beds filled with grass to look like sleeping people and crawled away into the nearby tall grass to sleep. Once again they posted guards to watch over the camp.

In the middle of the night, warriors snuck into the camp and stabbed their spears into the fake sleepers. When they realized they had been fooled, they ran away, thinking that the trick was an ambush.

The continual obstacles and constant threat of harm from tribal warriors was too much for the porters. "We must go home," cried all the porters in the morning. "If we do not, we will all die!"

Reluctantly, Livingstone agreed. They had traveled nearly two hundred miles up the lake shore, but still the water to the north seemed to run on into the sky. They had not yet discovered a river flowing east to the ocean . . . on the other hand, they had not proved that a river didn't exist, either.

As they sailed back down the lake, Chuma noticed that the doctor said very little. Clearly he was discouraged by their failure. It made Chuma sad, too. They had come so far—for nothing! The more the doctor had talked about finding a river going to the ocean so he could start a mission, the more the boy had wanted to help make it happen. Like Livingstone, Chuma had been happy when they had a good day traveling or made friends with the local tribespeople, and he was sad when things went wrong.

Chuma thought about this as the boat creaked under the sail. Just last summer he was a sheepherder. Now he was traveling with the white doctor who wanted to stop the evil slavers. He didn't understand everything the doctor said, but he did know that Livingstone wanted all the tribes to live peacefully with one another. He was a good man. Chuma was only a boy . . . but he wanted to help Livingstone, too.

As they journeyed southward on the lake, the explorers avoided the areas where they had encountered problems before. But they faced a new problem: the weather. One morning Wikatani said, "The big winds are coming; we must not go out on the lake today."

Everyone looked up at the sky and wondered what he saw. While there was some haze in the sky, the sun was bright, and the day seemed like any other. If anything, the breeze was a little lighter than usual. "What do you mean?" laughed Livingstone. "It's a beautiful day." He proceeded to get ready to shove off.

Chuma knew that Wikatani had gone out frequently on Lake Shirwa with his father, and was probably more familiar with the weather in the area than anyone in the group. But even Chuma thought his friend was mistaken.

"The windy season is starting," Wikatani insisted. "It will blow today, and it will blow so hard that we could sink." The boy was truly frightened and at first refused to get in the boat, even after everyone else had climbed in and actually pushed off from shore.

From a few yards off shore Doctor Livingstone called back, "Come on, Wikatani. We don't want to leave you, but we *are* sailing this morning. So get in the boat."

With fearful eyes the boy waded out to the waiting craft and reluctantly climbed in. He actually shook with fright as he sat down in the bottom of the boat and looked up at the sky.

They traveled almost two hours under a good breeze and sunny skies when suddenly the wind shifted. Within minutes it turned into a gale. The waves in the shallow lake grew enormously, driving the little boat toward an angry surf crashing on a rocky shore. Livingstone and the boys immediately lowered the sail, and the men began to row with all their might. But still the wind drove them directly toward the rocks. Finally, Livingstone ordered, "Drop anchor! It's the only way to keep us out of those breakers."

But with the anchor out, the waves broke over the side and filled the boat, threatening to sink it. Everyone bailed out the water as fast as possible. Chuma

and Wikatani had nothing to scoop water, so they used their hands. Hour after hour the little band struggled to keep the boat afloat. Many times Chuma clung terrified to the side of the boat, sure it was going to tip over or sink, and they would all drown.

But six hours later the wind finally slackened; exhausted, the men rowed slowly away from the rocks and beached on a sandy shore.

From then on, Doctor Livingstone listened to Wikatani's advice when he said a wind was coming up. As a result, they spent many miserable days on shore waiting for the waves to go down. But in Chuma's mind, it was a lot better than bailing water.

On October 26, they arrived again at the south end of the lake. That night as they all sat dejectedly around the fire, Wikatani said, "Doctor, now can we try going south to Lake Shirwa?"

A hush fell over the whole group as everyone's eyes turned toward the doctor. Finally, he said, "All right. In the morning we'll find a place to hide the boat and set out on foot."

But in the morning, the doctor and the boys awoke to a terrible shock. During the night all the porters had run away.

Chapter 12

Home and Beyond

WHAT WILL WE DO NOW?" asked Chuma.

"Well, we can always sail the boat by ourselves," said the doctor. "Even one man can sail it."

"But you said we'd go to Lake Shirwa," said Wikatani.

Livingstone laughed wryly. "It would be foolish without any porters. They took the guns. What if we were attacked?"

"But Doctor, you said you didn't want to use guns, anyway," protested Chuma.

"I don't, but it's never good to appear weak in the face of danger."

"Won't God protect us if we are doing His work?" asked Chuma sincerely.

The doctor turned away from the boys and looked

north across the lake shimmering in its morning light. When he turned back, he sighed deeply. "I'm not sure I know what God's work for me is anymore," he confessed, pulling the ends of his moustache. "I was so sure, but . . . everything I try seems to fail."

He got up and set to building a fire. When it was crackling its comfort into the chill air, he turned to the boys again. "I guess there is still one thing I know to do." He looked into the fire and tossed a twig at it. "I should take you boys home. You've risked your lives for me, and even though I may not be able to save all of Africa from this evil slave trade, I can pay my debt to you. Let's go."

The boys were elated. But first they rowed the boat up a small stream flowing into the lake until they came to a marsh where they concealed the boat among tall reeds.

"There," said Livingstone. "Unless someone knows right where it is or comes on it accidentally, it'll never be found. I may not come back this way to explore Lake Nyassa again. But if I do, I'll have a boat." And his craggy face broke into a grin.

Then the doctor and the two boys waded out of the marsh and headed south.

❖ ❖ ❖ ❖

It was near sunset three days later when they came over a hill and saw in the distance the shining mirror of Lake Shirwa. This country was more open—rolling hills, groves of forest, and open grassland.

The three travelers were hungry and bone-tired. Along the way, they had avoided other people and all villages. They did not want to announce their presence. But that also meant that they had no way of getting more food except for what they could gather along the trail.

And the land to the north of Lake Shirwa had not been free from warfare, either. From a distance they had seen burned villages, and on the trails they frequently came across a warning sign: a skull atop a spear that had been driven into the ground.

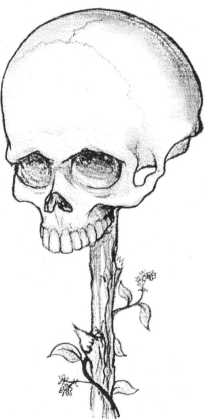

But as they looked at their lake in the distance, Chuma asked, "Can we keep on going so we can get home tonight?"

Livingstone surveyed the lake glistening in the distance and then looked at how close the sun was to the horizon. "The lake is still several miles away. Where's your village?"

"Around the lake,

on the west shore," offered Wikatani.

"It's a pretty big lake; it could take quite a while to get there. I think we ought to wait until morning."

Though the boys were greatly disappointed, they did not complain. They knew the doctor was very tired and had already taken great risks in bringing them this far. But when they made camp, the boys could hardly sleep.

"I wonder if our sheep all wandered back to the village?" whispered Chuma as they stared up at the bright stars.

"Our sheep? They are too dumb. If someone didn't go out and round them up, they'd wander right off the earth."

"You think our families think we are dead?"

"Probably," said Wikatani. "Won't they be surprised when we come marching in?"

"I'm going to have my mother make a big feast for Doctor Livingstone." Chuma could hear the man already snoring softly near them.

"Maybe my father will assign some men to be new porters for him," said Wikatani.

In their excitement, the boys left unspoken any fears they had about the Manganja boast that all the villages around Lake Shirwa had been burned out. After all it was just a boast; the Manganja had been trying to frighten them.

Finally, they dropped off to sleep. But they were up early in the morning, and, with the doctor in tow, they covered the distance to the lake shore while the air was still cool.

"Look," shouted Wikatani. "That's our village across the lake. See the white strip of beach and the little trail of smoke rising in the air. My mother is probably baking bread for breakfast."

Several times the doctor had to urge the boys to slow down as they traveled around the edge of the lake. After they had gone about five miles, Chuma pointed out that they were now on the trail that they often used when they took the sheep to pasture.

In another quarter hour, he said to the doctor, "Right down there, that is where the Red Caps got us."

"They tied me up," said Wikatani, "and broke a Manganja spear and shot one of our sheep."

"And I came running through the shallows to help him," said Chuma. "But an-other Red Cap was waiting for me, and he had a gun."

A few min-utes later, when the boys came in sight of their village, they began to race each other for home. Chuma was two strides behind Wikatani when Wikatani suddenly

stopped short. Chuma ran ahead in glee, looking back over his shoulder as he shot past his friend. But Wikatani was staring strangely ahead. Chuma also slowed down as he looked down the hill toward the village.

Something was wrong. There were no canoes on the beach. Some of the houses had been knocked down, some burned. Chuma pushed the panic away and forced himself to walk. There were no joyful sounds of children shouting and playing. No dogs came out to bark at them. But the village was not deserted. A few people could still be seen moving from hut to hut.

Again he began to run. He tore past the old sheep pen. There were no sheep in it. *Of course, someone else is out herding them*, he reassured himself. He turned right after the first house. Its thatched roof was caving in. In the doorway of the next house sat a strange woman. *Who's she? I know all my neighbors. I know everyone in the village*, he thought. *Maybe she's a visitor.* His own house was next, but as Chuma rounded the corner of his neighbor's house, he faced a burned-out pile of rubble. Half of one mud wall was still standing, and a few roof beams lay haphazardly against it like a blackened logjam on a river after a spring flood.

He turned to the right and left. The only building belonging to Chuma's family that still stood was their corn crib. He ran over to it and around to the door, thinking his family might be taking shelter within, but that whole side was knocked out. Not one single ear of corn remained.

"Mother! Father!" Chuma yelled. "Mother, where is everyone?" He ran to the next house—just a hut, really—but it was completely empty. He ran on from house to house. All had been badly damaged; many had been burned to the ground.

Panic completely engulfed him. He ran up behind an old grandmother—finally, someone he knew! He grabbed her, and spun her around. "Where is my mother?" he demanded. But the old woman didn't say a word. She just stared at him as if he were a ghost.

He ran to the other side of the village to Wikatani's house. As he approached, he saw with relief that it was standing and that people were home. Wikatani was standing outside, talking to someone standing in the dark doorway.

"Where's my family?" he insisted as he skidded to a stop.

Wikatani turned to him with horror on his face. "They're dead. Almost everyone is dead!" His voice came out in a high-pitched whisper.

"No. It can't be! Who are these people?" Chuma pushed past the woman standing in the doorway of Wikatani's house. He looked around. There were several others in the dark interior, but he recognized no one. "Who are these people?" he demanded as he came back out into the blinding sun.

"They say they are my cousins," said Wikatani. "They're from another village . . . over the hills." He pointed back toward the north.

"But what has happened?"

The boys looked at each other in silence. Finally, the woman standing in the doorway spoke up. "The Ajawa had many great victories, but then the battle turned and the Manganja overran this village. Many warriors from our village in the hills came down to help, but we were too late."

Wikatani sat down in the dust and began to rock back and forth, moaning quietly. Chuma just stood there. He knew that war killed people, but he had refused to believe that his family might die, not even when the Manganja man had said that the villages around Lake Shirwa had been defeated.

"But all are not dead," said the woman as she came out and put her hand on Wikatani's shoulder. "Your little brother is still alive."

At first it seemed that Wikatani had not heard. Then he looked up slowly and said, "What?"

"I said, your little brother is alive."

"Where?"

"He is with your uncle, down at the lake."

Wikatani jumped up and ran toward the water. Chuma turned and followed along slowly, walking as though he were in a dream. Suddenly Doctor Livingstone was walking beside him. The white man put his arm around the boy's shoulder and pulled him close.

At the lake front, Chuma and the doctor stood at a distance while Wikatani and his little brother hugged each other and cried. They stood there in silence a very long time. Finally, the doctor said,

"You know, Chuma, you *could* come with me."

✧ ✧ ✧

That night the two boys went for a walk along the lake shore. They followed the path they had taken with the sheep that fateful day and stopped again at the point where they had been ambushed. They sat on the sand thinking about all that had happened in the last months.

"Chuma, when you get back to the mission, try to talk to Dauma again. Tell her that I'll never forget her kindness to us."

"Without her, we might have died," agreed Chuma.

Soon a new moon rose. It was nothing more than a golden fingernail of light, but it laid down a shimmering path across the placid, black waters.

"The doctor saved our lives, too," added Wikatani.

"Yes," said Chuma. "He's been like a father to us."

"You know, I think he knew what we might find here . . . and he didn't have to bring us back."

"But I'm glad he did. I had to know."

"Me, too."

Somewhere in the distance a hyena howled its hideous laugh. In a few minutes Wikatani continued. "You once said that if our families were dead, you would become a Christian and stay with the doctor. Is that why you are going with him?"

Chuma thought before answering. "No. I became a Christian when I still thought our families were safe . . . and I would still be a Christian even if the doctor hadn't offered for me to go with him."

"Yes. I think you would. And I believe in Jesus, too. Do you think he would baptize me before you go?"

Chuma grinned at his friend. "Of course! Ask him—first thing in the morning!"

"But I wish I could help the doctor, too," said Wikatani wistfully. "He *is* doing a great work, even if he can't see the benefits."

"That's true," agreed Chuma. "How else would we have heard about Jesus? Someone had to come tell us."

A slight breeze turned the path of moonlight on the lake into a field of glittering diamonds. Again, Wikatani broke the silence. "I just wish I could go with you."

"Me, too. But you need to take care of your brother, and we don't want our village to die out."

"No. I guess not." After a moment Wikatani turned to Chuma. "You wouldn't desert the doctor like those porters did, would you? Promise me!"

Chuma grasped Wikatani's wrist, as his friend's hand clasped his own wrist in a sign of friendship.

"As long as God gives me the strength and courage, I will remain with Doctor Livingstone and help him in his work," Chuma vowed. "You can count on that, my friend."

Chapter 13

Epilogue

CHUMA REMAINED at Doctor Livingstone's side for seven more years of missionary exploration in Africa's interior. When the good doctor died from exhaustion and fever, Chuma and others carefully preserved his body and then carried it across half of Africa to the coast where it could be sent by ship back to England for burial.

Chuma was also invited to England to help tell the story of Livingstone's life to all those who had admired and supported his great work.

Though Livingstone never had the privilege of seeing the fruit of his efforts, he opened the way for hundreds of missionaries to enter central Africa and establish mission stations there. One of the most important was located on Lake Nyassa and named

Livingstonia. And within fifteen years of his death, through the influence of the Gospel, as well as other factors, the slave trade was brought to an end in central Africa.

More About David Livingstone

DAVID LIVINGSTONE WAS BORN on March 19, 1813, on an island off the coast of Scotland. He grew up in a Christian home where his father was a tea merchant.

After receiving a degree in medicine from Glasgow University in 1840, Livingstone became connected with the London Missionary Society. With the Society's support he went to South Africa in 1841. He ventured north by lumbering ox-wagon on a ten-week trip. But what he saw troubled him. The mission stations he visited seemed more interested in creating comfortable British outposts than pressing on to reach the unreached peoples of the interior. He also discovered that some of the missionaries were racist about the very people they were trying to reach with the Gospel. They did not think the Africans were suited for much more than servants or field hands.

Livingstone's complaints to the mission headquarters earned him the disapproval of some, and he was not granted permission for an extended missionary journey for several years. So he spent his time learning everything he could about Africa and its people. He became convinced that when English missionaries founded a mission station, they should set about training African converts to take it over as soon as possible. He quickly mastered several African languages and learned the customs of the people.

On one shorter foray into the bush, Livingstone was attacked and severely mauled by a lion. It took months for him to recover, and the injuries to his shoulder bothered him the rest of his life. However, while he was recovering, he got to know Mary Moffat, the daughter of Dr. Robert Moffat, Bible translator and mission director.

Shortly after they were married in 1844, the Livingstones set out to establish a new mission station on the frontier. From there it was Livingstone's intention to make journeys deep into Africa to reach people who had never heard the Gospel before.

This he did in three dramatic expeditions.

The first expedition extended north across the eastern edge of the Kilahari Desert to the River Zouga and then west; he become the first white man to see Lake Nagami in 1849. He then went on to reach the Zambezi River in 1851.

Before long he came to realize that he wasn't an evangelist but had been called by God to explore and open up new areas for other missionaries to follow. Between 1853 and 1856 he made a most remarkable Trans-Africa journey, first out to the west coast, then back across Africa, down the Zambezi River to sight the Victoria Falls, and then on to the east coast.

It was on this first journey that he became aware of the devastation of the slave trade in Africa. When he returned to England in 1856, he was honored by the Royal Geographic Society as a major explorer and commissioned by the government to return to Africa as a British Consul.

He went back to Africa on his second expedition and started up the Zambezi River by river boat. There he intended to establish Christian mission stations in the hope of spreading the Gospel and stopping the slave trade. That situation provides the setting for this story.

Though greatly simplified, this story follows the events of the Zambezi expedition with the following exceptions: (1) It is only conjecture that Chuma and Wikatani were the spark the Red Caps used to ignite the tribal war. (2) While at least two freed slaves accompanied Livingstone in his attempt to contact the Ajawa chiefs on his Nyassa exploration, they are not named. (3) Livingstone's rescue from the Shire River is fiction, though he had an equally close call with death earlier when coming down the Zambezi River. (4) Chuma and Wikatani did not return to their homeland for another five years. For the sake of this story, the time frame was condensed. What actually happened in the meantime was that Livingstone's second expedition came to a tragic end.

Livingstone's wife as well as the wife of Bishop Mackenzie and some other women came to join the men at the mission station. However, when Livingstone was away exploring Lake Nyassa, the bishop made a canoe trip on which he foolishly carried most of the mission's medicines. The canoe capsized and all the medicines were lost. By the time Livingstone got back, everyone was so sick with malaria that the bishop and all the women died—including Mary Moffat Livingstone.

Shortly after that, even in the middle of his great grief, Livingstone came across an official dispatch that conclusively proved that the Portuguese were involved in the slave trade. He sent off this proof to England, thinking the government would put international pressure on Portugal to stop the trade. However, it was more important to England to maintain good relations with Portugal at that time than to embarrass their ally by exposing Portugal's violation of the treaty. To avoid any further "incidents," England ordered Livingstone out of Africa.

Heartbroken and discouraged, Livingstone withdrew, vowing to return at his own expense as soon as he could. Rather than allow his riverboat (it was his third one by this time) to fall into the hands of the slave traders, he sailed it across the open sea to India. Chuma and Wikatani—as well as some other African and white sailors—volunteered to accompany him on this wild and dangerous voyage in which all nearly lost their lives. In India, Livingstone enrolled Chuma and Wikatani in a mission school and sold his boat before returning home to England.

Several years later Dauma was reported to be a fine teacher in a mission school in South Africa. She had been among some of women and children Livingstone brought down the river to safety on his boat before he sailed to India. He arranged for them to be cared for at the mission station on the island of Zanzibar.

Three years after leaving Chuma and Wikatani in India, Livingstone returned to take them back to Africa for his third expedition. They faithfully accompanied him until they arrived in their homeland. There Wikatani stayed—probably to get married—but Chuma continued on with Livingstone.

Livingstone went deep into the interior of Africa and lost all contact with the outside world. Many thought him dead until the *New York Herald* sent newspaper reporter Henry Stanley on an expedition to find him or bring back conclusive news of his death. In March 1871, Stanley started his search from Zanzibar. In the fall he finally located Livingstone. The doctor was sick and out of supplies, but in good spirits. Their meeting is remembered by Stanley's famous words: "Doctor Livingstone, I presume?"

Though grateful for the visit and the fresh medicines and supplies, Livingstone would not come out of Africa. So Stanley returned to world-wide fame for having found the great missionary/explorer.

When Livingstone died on April 30, 1873, Chuma and some other faithful companions carefully wrapped and embalmed his body and carried it to the coast. There, Chuma went with the body to England where Livingstone was buried with great honor. Chuma met with the Queen and toured the country telling others about the expeditions of Livingstone.